THE TRUTH
ABOUT KATIE

By Merrill J. Davies

Martin Sisters Publishing

Published by

Martin Sisters Publishing, LLC

www. martinsisterspublishing. com

DEDICATION

This book is dedicated to my husband Bill, who has always encouraged and supported me in all my writing efforts. I also want to acknowledge my friend Cathy Aiken-Freeman, a Beta Reader, who gave her time to read the story and give feedback; and finally one of my best friends, Martha Heneisen, who took many hours away from her own writing to give a careful reading of the manuscript.

"…I will go to the king even though it is against the law. And if I perish, I perish."

~ Esther 4:16

CHAPTER 1

"Hello," said the vaguely familiar voice, "Mom?"

Picturing the small blond-haired girl standing in the faraway kitchen holding the phone made Agatha's breath catch in a way she hadn't expected. At that moment, she realized that she was not really Agatha after all. Her arm seldom bothered her, but it was aching today, reminding her of the slight deformity of her left arm.

"Hi, Abby," she said, shifting the phone to her good arm, so she could hear the small voice better. Scenes began to flash before her eyes: Abby at her first birthday, Abby in first grade at Royal Oaks School, Abby trying to explain why she was in trouble with her teacher for talking too much. Abby had always been headstrong.

"Where are you?" Abby asked, in a voice that seemed cautiously interested.

"Well, right now I'm in Nashville, but I'll be home soon," said Agatha. She imagined herself getting off I-75 at the London, Kentucky, exit and driving on West-80 toward

Somerset. She saw the narrow road as it wound down toward where she turned toward Laurel Creek or progressed on toward the home that she and Seth had bought when Abby was a baby.

There was a long pause, and then Abby said, "Well, I guess I'll see you then. I'd better go now. Bye." She hung up.

Agatha realized that Abby had grown up a lot in the time Agatha had been gone, but she was still only eight. She sounded different, like someone Agatha didn't really know.

Agatha sat there for a long time after the click of the phone and the dial tone had begun before she hung up the receiver, wondering if she should have agreed when Seth asked if she would speak to Abby. She imagined Abby as she had been two years ago at age six. She could see the confident look in her face, the mischievous twinkle in her eyes, her energetic movement as she bounded across the kitchen in her new UK sweatshirt. Was the sink full of dishes? Were toys and clothes strewn through the house? Was dirty laundry on the floor of the laundry room?

Sadness overwhelmed her and she began to sob. For the first time in over a year, she allowed herself to feel, to ask the unspoken questions that had haunted her for so long. What memories lurked underneath the calm, logical demeanor that had dominated her exterior persona for years? When she had reached a point where she had to confront her fears or run, she had run. For the last year, she had tried to use logic and approach her problem by seeking the help of a professional.

When Dr. Burton, her counselor, had suggested that she call home and face her past, she had agreed. But it hurt to admit how miserably she had failed her family. She wanted to back out of the agreement. Yet she yearned for her children. She wanted to see them, to hold them, to beg them to forgive her.

Exhausted from weeping, Agatha glanced at the clock. It was almost time for her to be at work. She had promised Greta Burns to fill in for her tonight at O'Neill's Fast and Friendly Food Restaurant. Greta had become her best friend in the last few months, and she felt a little guilty. What would her friends think if they knew the truth? Greta seldom asked a favor.

"It's Mom's birthday, and I'd really like to take her out for dinner without having to rush off to work," Greta had said.

"As you know, you are my only friend, so I don't have anything else to do anyway." Agatha had laughed.

"What about Jennifer Ford?"

"Married," said Agatha.

"Yeah, I know. But still I thought you two were friends."

"We are, and she was very helpful in orienting me to the job, but since then, we haven't spent much time together."

"That was a good thing, too, because you know how I am— not nearly as organized and serious as Jennifer. You might have never learned to hold up the high standards that our local establishment is built upon."

"What do you mean?" asked Agatha.

"Well you know, our managers are all scared to death that all these new chain restaurants will take away all our business, so they harp on 'high standards' all the time."

Greta had worked there two years before Agatha came and was actually very helpful when Agatha first came to work. But it was unusual that they became friends. Greta seemed the exact opposite of Agatha in many ways. Her blonde curly hair and her tendency to overdo the make-up made her seem a little like the stereotypical blonde. However, something clicked with the two girls, and they often chatted before, after, and during work. So when one of them needed a favor, the other usually accommodated. Agatha made good tips and she needed the money now, especially if she planned to go back home next month. *Home.* Where is home? She went to her bedroom to get ready for work.

She looked at herself in the mirror. Her long legs and slim body didn't look bad in the tailored uniform. Her dark brown hair curling around her face made her look younger than she really was. She looked much like all the other servers at the restaurant, except a little older, and she hoped a little more elegant. No one had ever suspected that she was not Agatha Kingsley, the career waitress. Greta was always talking about going back to school. She would find a flier about Belmont College or maybe an advertisement for a business school and show it to the other girls. She'd be all excited at the possibility. Her immature attitude about college always annoyed Agatha, and she would say, "Okay, if that's what you want."

Greta would say, "Yeah, I know you've never thought of doing anything else, but me, one 'a these days I'm gonna be somebody. Lord, you won't even recognize me, honey." Greta's attitude seemed naïve to Agatha.

Once, frustrated with her friend, Agatha responded, "There's a lot more to life than college."

"How would you know?" Greta responded.

Agatha said nothing.

Later, Greta had said, "I know you think I'm a country hick and wouldn't even make it in college, but I was a good student in high school, and if Mama hadn't married that sorry husband and let him take all our insurance money Daddy left when he died, I'd a gone to college long time ago."

Thinking of Greta's words, Agatha remembered the small rural community where she grew up. Suddenly she realized that

Greta reminded her of that little community. That may have been both the reason she resonated with the young girl and the reason she was often frustrated with her.

Agatha grabbed her jacket and her purse, and headed out the door, making sure to lock it behind her. Her red Honda Accord was old but so far it had been reliable. She had bought it soon after she moved to Nashville and got the job at O'Neill's. She had been so glad to get a job on Nolensville Road, not too far from East Iris Drive, where she had found the little house to rent. It was a two-bedroom, yellow house with white shutters. It seemed a lifetime ago since she'd moved in.

She drove slowly, knowing that she had plenty of time before she had to be at work, and she needed time to think. She was beginning to be bored with her routine here in Nashville. That was probably why Dr. Burton had encouraged her to face up to her real life; he had sensed her restlessness the last few weeks. Agatha remembered exactly when she became aware that she needed a change. It was one evening as she and Greta were leaving work. They had worked together all evening and were talking about where to go after work. Some of the "gang" was going out for a while, and Greta suggested going with them.

"I don't think so," said Agatha. "I'm headed home."

"You don't have a date with Kirk, do you?" asked Greta, a note of concern in her voice.

"No," said Agatha.

"Well, what's wrong with you? Too good to go with us?" teased one of the girls.

"No, I just don't feel like going anywhere," said Agatha. But the jab hit home. She really did not fit in at all with these people. Greta seemed to understand a little, but she was comfortable with these girls and enjoyed hanging out with them. First, Agatha, at age forty, was a good bit older than most of these girls, and by the time she finished her shift, her left arm was always extremely tired and usually hurting. But it was more than that. They had a certain mentality. To Agatha, they seemed shallow, immature, and extremely materialistic. She wasn't exactly critical of them. How could she be after what she had done? However, when she listened to them, she just could see nothing of significance in their conversations. They made her want to get back home and read a book or watch the History Channel on television. Finally, she convinced Greta to go on with the girls and she went home by herself. That night she admitted to herself that she would eventually have to do something besides work at O'Neill's.

When she went to see her counselor, she barely had time to mention her need before he was encouraging her to act on it. He felt that if she were to move forward she first had to look backward and face her past. It took two more sessions before she had worked out a plan for doing that. Now she had taken the first step. It was a small step, and in taking it, she did not feel she had accomplished much. In fact, in some ways she wished she had not made the call. But it was done.

As soon as she entered the restaurant, she knew it would be a busy night. Waiters and servers were running around like crazy and it was only five o'clock.

"Great, you're finally here!" said Jan. Agatha ignored Jan's implication that she was late, which she wasn't. Jan was an assistant manager, was always in a hurry, and usually showed up ten minutes early, just so she could make others seem late.

The manager saw Agatha and thanked her for filling in, telling her that a large group on a tour bus was due any minute and he wanted her to help get the tables ready for them.

Agatha left her purse and jacket in her personal locker and then got right to work, thankful for the busy night, which would keep her thoughts off the challenge she was facing in the next few weeks. The sound of her daughter's small voice had kept echoing in her ears ever since she hung up the phone this afternoon.

Members of the large touring group were mostly senior citizens. Several of them had special diets or were just plain meticulous eaters. Agatha was very busy and had little time to think all evening. When the shift was over, she rubbed her arm for a moment before retrieving her things from her locker and heading home for the night.

Agatha awoke the next morning with a splitting headache. Her thoughts immediately went to her conversation with the girls last night. She remembered Greta's question about a date with Kirk. As she sat up, she tried to remember what she had been dreaming just prior to waking. Oh! She had been trying to explain something to Kirk Stone. Then she realized that she was really thinking about yesterday's phone call in her dream. Yes, of course she would have to deal with Kirk.

Lately she had got the impression that Kirk thought she was his girlfriend, and she had to clear that up, even if she didn't go back home. She had met Kirk just after she started work in Nashville. He was tall and lanky, with an unruly shock of blond hair that always looked as if he had just come out of a windstorm. He worked for one of the recording companies, but she never figured out exactly what he did. He didn't scout for new recording stars, but he helped entertain them when they came to town. She had met him through the owner of O'Neill's, when Kirk had come there to make arrangements to bring a group there for dinner and the owner had allowed her to get the details. During the conversation, Agatha had mentioned that she was new in town and was moving into a house that week. Somehow, Kirk ended up volunteering to help her, saying he had a truck and could pick up a sofa she had bought. After that he had done several little odd jobs for her, and they had seen each other off and on for the last several months, but their encounters were always centered on something one of them needed help with as friends. He had never called her and asked her out to dinner or anything that would be considered a date.

As she thought about telling Kirk that she might be leaving Nashville, something more than just the normal dread lurked in her mind. It was something Kirk had said which she could not remember, but it suggested a violent nature that she had refused to acknowledge at the time. She couldn't put her finger on why she was so reluctant to tell him about her plans.

She met Kirk for lunch during his break between clients. She knew it was not a particularly good time to talk to him about leaving Nashville, but she needed to tell someone, and Kirk had really been a friend to her. But how should she begin?

"Kirk, you know I've been seeing a counselor the last few months…"

"Yes, I know. What sort of kooky advice has he given you?" he said, laughing. Kirk never seemed to have much respect for the psychiatric profession.

"Nothing exactly. I just feel that I need to tell you something. I may have to leave Nashville in a few weeks, and I wanted you to know," said Agatha quietly.

14

"Now I know he's been giving you kooky advice. I guess he's told you to get away from me. Is that right?" said Kirk, moving closer to her and grinning.

"Oh, no, Kirk, nothing like that," Agatha said, becoming alarmed at the unexpected response from her friend. "No, I just need to deal with some things from my past. It has nothing to do with my friendship with you," she added reassuringly. "Why would you even think such a thing?"

"What sort of 'things'? I thought we were friends. Friends don't hide stuff from one another. So, tell me. What is it?" Kirk seemed a little edgy, but he was trying to hide it with humor.

She wished she had not mentioned leaving. "Well, I just need to go visit my family back in Alabama. That's all I can tell you at this time," Agatha said, hoping to end the conversation.

"Why are you so mysterious all of a sudden? You have never acted like this before. I have to tell you that you mean more to me than just being a friend," he said. He reached over and took her left hand. He looked at it a minute. "In fact," he said, "I kind of thought we were a couple."

She couldn't help moving her hand away, and she felt sure he could see the look of panic on her face, but neither one of them mentioned it.

Finally, she looked at him and said, "I'm sorry, Kirk, but I just wasn't prepared for that comment. You have been a wonderful friend to me, and I appreciate it. I'm just not ready to commit to a serious relationship right now. I've got a lot of issues to work on first."

"Well, okay then," said Kirk. He was no longer agitated as he had been earlier, but there was something almost sinister in the way he looked at her. Soon it was time for them to depart, and they said little until he walked her out to her car and she left.

When Agatha got home her answering machine was blinking to indicate a new message. She was always excited when she had a message, because this was the first time she had owned an answering machine. But most all her co-workers had one when she moved here, and they insisted that she just "had to have one." She pushed the button.

"Hello, Agatha, or whatever you're calling yourself now. This is Seth. You may have noticed that I have not changed my name, but I'm not exactly the man I was two years ago either. I need to talk to you. Please call me as soon as possible." Agatha sat there and thought about the message. His voice sounded somewhat familiar, but there was no emotion—not anger, not joy, not anticipation, just flat. Not the Seth Johnson she remembered.

In her mind she replayed their conversation the day she made the call. He had answered casually, almost jovial, but when she said his name and told him who she was, the phone was silent on the other end for several seconds.

"Katie? Katie? Is it you? Where are you?"

"I'm in Nashville," she said beginning to panic.

"Are you all right? What happened to you?" She could hear the emotion and concern in his voice. She imagined that he was wondering if she'd been kidnapped or something.

As she began to try to explain to him about what had happened, she realized how ridiculous it all must sound. The more they talked, she could tell that some anger was replacing the concern his voice had expressed at first. She heard a child in the background saying something, and then without warning, he had said, "Here's Abby—she wants to talk to you." And when Abby finished and hung up, it was a relief, but now the message on the answering machine reminded her that the conversation had just begun.

Maybe she had waited too long to try to go back. She went to bed with a sinking feeling that she was in deep trouble, and that there was no way out.

CHAPTER 2

Agatha worked a long shift and her feet were hurting. All she wanted to do was go home, soak her feet in hot water, and then curl up with a good book. Before she left work, she looked at her calendar. Oh no! She had an appointment with Dr. Burton at 4:00 o'clock, which gave her exactly twenty minutes to get there and it was pouring rain.

As she pulled out on Gallatin Road, she realized she should have taken another route, but it was too late by then, so she just hoped she'd make it within a few minutes of her appointment time. Dr. Burton was usually on time and expected his patients to be on time also.

The session began well with Dr. Burton asking her about work and a few other rather unimportant issues that they had talked about the last time she had been there. Then he asked if she had "made the call."

"Yes, I did," she said without emotion.

"And how did it go?" he asked.

"Okay, I guess," she responded.

"Would you like to tell me about it?"

"Not really," she replied stubbornly.

After a few more questions with similar answers, Dr. Burton said, "Come on, Agatha, I can't help you if you refuse to talk to me. Just tell me what's bothering you."

"Well, for one thing, I don't think I'm ready to do this. I just want to stop and stay here and forget about my past. I'm doing okay without dealing with all that," she said sullenly.

"But you said you'd already called. Isn't that a start? Can you just act like it didn't happen?" asked the doctor. He was looking at her as if she was an idiot. She did not like him at all at this moment. He leaned back in his chair, and although he sat beside her (supposedly to make her feel comfortable, on the same level), she did not feel comfortable at all. She felt as if he were judging her, looking down at her pathetic life and finding it just that, pathetic.

"I don't know. All I know is that I'm just not ready to go back and I feel trapped between two lives, so I choose to stay in this one."

"Can you do that? It seems to me that once you've made the first move you need to go forward; otherwise you'll never make any progress. You've got to face this double life you've been living, Agatha. You don't necessarily have to go back to your old life, but you need to face up to it. Admit what happened and make a decision about where you want to go from here."

"Let's just talk about something else," she said suddenly.

"Okay, what do you want to talk about?"

"I don't know, just pick another topic."

"Well, how about your relationship with Kirk? How's that going? Is he still 'just a friend,' as you've always insisted?" He said, grinning slightly. For some reason that topic was not any more appealing than the last one.

"I really don't want to discuss Kirk either," she said

"Okay, what about work? How's your friend Greta doing? Are you still friends with her?" he asked tentatively.

"Yes, we're still friends, but I don't know anything to say about her. She's okay, I guess."

Suddenly Dr. Burton stood. "Agatha," he said, "I think that until you decide whether you want to face up to your life and make some progress with your parallel lives, there's really nothing I can do for you. You seem to have just decided to quit. When you decide to move forward, I'll be glad to listen and help guide you in your journey, but if you refuse to take charge of your life I can't really help you."

"I AM taking charge!" Agatha almost shouted at him. "I'm deciding to do nothing about going back to my old life, and you have no right to tell me I have to!"

"Okay, but don't be surprised if you are forced into facing your past now that you've made that call. And remember that it was your decision to make the call, not mine," Dr. Burton said. "And know that I'm here if you need me."

"I don't need you to push me into things I'm not ready for," she mumbled as she slammed the door on her way out.

She drove home with her mind spinning. Kirk was angry with her, her therapist was through with her, and she hated both of them! On some level, she saw the logic of what Dr. Burton had said, but she just was not ready to go back and try to explain all that had happened since she left. She didn't really think she could even if she tried.

When she finally got back home, she was too tired to soak her feet or read a book. All she wanted to do was go to sleep.

She saw the blinking light again on her answering machine, but afraid it was another call from Seth, she just ate a snack and got ready for bed instead of listening to it.

On Thursday morning, Agatha slept until ten since she did not go into work until three. She drank her coffee slowly while watching the news and then fixed a big breakfast of pancakes. While she was eating she remembered her answering machine message and reached over to push the <u>play</u> button.

After a buzzing sound, the voice said, "Seth again here. I guess you aren't checking messages this week. This is the second time I've called. I've decided to make a trip to Nashville to see you. You said you work at O'Neill's on Gallatin Road. I'll be there sometime Saturday afternoon. If you're not there, I'll get your address from them. Unless, of course you want to call and give me your address." Click.

Agatha's throat was dry. She tried to swallow. She stood up and walked around the room. She thought about what it would be like for Seth to be in this room. She thought about what it would be like for him to show up at the restaurant. No, she couldn't let him do that! She just couldn't. She began to dial his number.

CHAPTER 3

"Lord, why did you want to meet here?" asked Greta, as she got out of her car at the park Sunday. "This place looks like it's fallin' apart. You said you had something you wanted to talk about." A look of concern came over her face. "You and Kirk aren't getting serious, are you?"

"No…at least I'm not. I'm not so sure about Kirk, but that's not what I want to talk about. I have something more important to tell you, and I hope you won't be angry with me for deceiving you." Agatha approached Greta's car and motioned toward a picnic area that was virtually deserted on that late October afternoon. She felt a slight chill as she walked around the car. "Let's sit over here."

Greta's face showed concern. "Lord, Agatha, I ain't never seen you like this. Just tell me what's goin' on."

"Nothing's going on exactly." Agatha took a deep breath. How should she begin? She realized Greta was staring at her, waiting. "I've got to confess something to you."

"Okay. Go ahead. I'm all ears," said Greta.

"I'm not who you think I am. My name's not really Agatha and I didn't move here from Birmingham."

Greta looked stunned. "Wh- What? What do you mean?"

"I can't tell you much, but I have to tell you that I have a husband, and he's likely to show up in Nashville soon, so you need to know."

"You mean you've lied to me all this time? How dare you allow me to confess all my troubles and stuff to you and you not be honest with me? What kind a friend are you?"

"Wait a minute, now...I never meant to hurt you. I just couldn't face my own life and had to invent one. I wanted to tell you, but I just couldn't tell anyone. No one here knows."

Greta stared at the picnic area and the swing sets a moment, and then said, "Well, did your husband beat you or something? 'Cause if he did I..."

"No...no, it wasn't anything like that," Agatha said slowly. "I really can't explain it. I just left."

"Man, how could you just leave? Who are you anyway, and where are you really from?"

Agatha sat there for a long time, looking across the park. It had been a long time since she had said her real name or even thought about it for that matter. It was as if she was pulling something out of a deep barrel that had been buried a long time and was getting rusty from lack of use.

Finally, she looked at Greta and said, "My name is Katie Johnson. Until I came to Nashville, I was an eighth grade language arts teacher in a small Southeastern Kentucky town." She hesitated and finally said, "And I have two young children."

"Lord! Now that *is* crazy! How could you just leave? Does anyone know where you are? I mean, you said your husband might come here, but has he known all the time? How did he find out where you are?"

"He only learned last week because I called him. I've been in counseling for several months and I came to the place where I thought I was ready to face my past, but now I'm not so sure. That's why I'm telling you. I think I may have made a mistake in calling my husband, but I guess I can't retract the call. Anyway, he called and said he was coming to Nashville. I managed to talk him into waiting a few weeks, but he will come eventually."

"And you just came here and acted like you were a waitress. You know it kind of makes me mad at you. I guess you were just laughing at all us uneducated hicks at the restaurant. Here you've been to college, yet when I talked about going back to school, you just acted like you weren't interested in doin' anything except working in a restaurant—like you were satisfied with being a waitress all your life."

"Well, I've tried the other, and I learned that things like that don't necessarily make you happy. There's more to life than how you make a living." However, Agatha had to admit she didn't really know exactly what that meant in her case, as she didn't seem to have figured out what made her happy at this point. "But I don't remember ever saying that I wanted to be a waitress all my life, either. I think you just decided that on your own. And I certainly wasn't laughing at you. I just didn't know what to say."

"Well, you sure didn't encourage me when I mentioned going back to school. You acted as if you didn't think that was a good idea," said Greta.

"It wasn't that I didn't like the idea. I just knew that being educated had not been a total solution for me, so I couldn't act as if I thought that would solve all your problems. Actually, I think it would be great for you to go back to school. I'm just not in a position to tell someone else what will work in life. I haven't even figured out how to manage my own life."

"Speaking of your life, what was it like? Tell me about your husband, your kids. What were they like?"

"My husband is a very stable, reliable guy. Nothing outstanding, but he was always good to me. Just didn't talk a lot. Sometimes I felt neglected, but I guess he did the best he could. He worked in insurance. He was a good father and all. And my kids, they are great kids...I...oh Greta, I feel so guilty." She began to cry.

Greta got up and came over to sit closer to Agatha. "I'm sorry, Agatha. I just don't know what to say. I'm in shock. I thought you were one person, and now you're someone else."

They sat in silence for a few minutes, Agatha sniffing and taking a tissue out of her pocket and wiping her eyes, and Greta staring across the park where some kids were playing on a swing. Greta finally stood and looked at Agatha.

"Is there anything I can do to help you?"

"No, I guess not. I've got myself in a terrible mess. I don't know how I got into it, why I got into it, or how to get out except to go back and face my family and try to learn what might have caused me to leave in the first place."

Greta looked at her watch. "Oh, I'm sorry Agatha, but I promised my mama I'd bring her dinner tonight, and it's almost five o'clock. I've got to go or I'll be late. She eats early."

"That's fine. I'm exhausted now anyway, and Greta, don't mention any of this to anyone else, okay?"

"I promise," said Greta, crossing her heart. "But promise me you'll let me know if you need someone to talk to. And I'm not mad at you. Lord, I can't afford to lose any friends right now. You're still my best friend, aren't you?"

"Of course. And you'll certainly be hearing from me."

Greta turned and left, and Agatha sat staring after her. Greta looked back once, and then got into her car and drove away.

Agatha sat there looking after her. Was Greta just using her mother as an excuse to get away? Was their friendship over, now that she knew Agatha had lied to her? She picked up her purse and walked slowly toward her car.

CHAPTER 4

Agatha felt relieved after her conversation with Greta, whom she had grown to trust. She left the park and drove around for a while, picked up a take-out dinner at the Chinese restaurant, went home and ate a leisurely meal. After channel surfing on television for a while, she finished her latest mystery novel, and finally went to sleep. She slept more soundly than she had in months.

She awoke late the next morning with a sense of need to complete some unfinished task. She realized that she needed to talk to Greta some more, to explain her life, to herself and to her friend. She realized that this was the first time since she left Kentucky that she had felt a need to talk about her experience. Maybe she was making progress after all. She poured some coffee, looked at the clock, and reached for the phone. She knew Greta was always up early to walk her dog, and was probably back by now, having her mid-morning breakfast and reading the newspaper.

"Good morning! How can I help you?" Greta's voice was cheerful and somewhat teasing.

Agatha guessed that Greta knew it would be her. It gave Agatha a feeling that her friend had accepted her as she was and that she could be trusted.

"I don't know if you can help me or not. I'm pretty messed up, I guess," said Agatha.

"Well, join the crowd. We're all messed up in different ways, but I think you're getting healthier by the day," said Greta. "After we talked yesterday, I got to thinking it must've taken a lot of courage for you to talk to me, and I really look up to you for that."

"I appreciate you listening, and I really need to talk to you some more. I wondered if you might come by tonight and have dinner with me. I have to make some pretty major decisions soon, and I need a sounding board before I make them."

"Sure," said Greta. "What time?"

"How about 7:00 o'clock? You don't have to work tonight, do you?"

"No. I'm free as a bird. Seven will be fine."

Agatha hung up the phone and was just about to get in the shower and get dressed, when her phone rang. She assumed it was Greta calling back to ask her something she had forgotten to ask. When she picked up, she was annoyed to hear Kirk's voice.

"Well," he began with an unmistakable edge in his voice, "I guess you're too busy to fool with me, now that you've got other friends to visit with."

Agatha remembered her last conversation with Kirk and she could tell that he remembered it too. At the same time, she couldn't quite understand his reference to "other friends."

"What do you mean?" she asked.

"What I mean is that I saw you and Greta at the park yesterday, having a leisurely afternoon. I also saw you coming out of the restaurant talking to some of the girls, so obviously you're quite popular now. And never even a phone call to your best friend or an apology for the way you practically dumped me the last time we talked."

"Have you been following me or something?" Agatha asked incredulously. She couldn't believe he had actually been watching her.

"Well, I thought you might call and apologize for the way you treated me, but after you didn't I was curious about what you were doing."

"I can't believe we're having this conversation. It's really none of your business who I talk to. I know we've been friends these last months, but that doesn't give you the right to monitor my other relationships," Agatha said firmly. She was furious.

"Hey," Kirk said, backing off a little, "I just called to see how you were. I didn't mean to get into an argument. Maybe I just had the wrong impression. I thought we were good friends, and maybe even a little more—at least I hoped—but anyway, you're right. I had no business snooping around. I apologize."

"Okay, I'm sorry too. I've just been a little up tight lately," Agatha conceded.

"Want to go to dinner tonight?" asked Kirk.

"I'm sorry, Kirk, but I already have plans for tonight," said Agatha.

"Okay then, see you around," said Kirk, sounding more like his usual cheerful self.

"Bye," said Agatha, as the other end of the phone went dead and the dial tone started.

By the time Greta arrived that evening, Agatha had made spaghetti, a big salad, and had the yeast rolls in the oven. She knew Greta would like that, and it was simple to do.

"Oh, something smells good!" said Greta as she walked in the door.

"Come on in and have a seat at the table. Dinner's almost ready," Agatha said, pulling out a chair and giving her friend a hug.

They made small talk during dinner and then both of them cleaned up the dishes. When they started into the living room, Greta said, "Okay, so tell me about Katie Johnson, the school teacher in Southeastern Kentucky."

"Yes. Well, I'm just going to have to tell it to you from the beginning, as I remember it these days. Some of it may not make any sense, but then some of it doesn't make any sense to me either. I know you'll probably think I'm an ungrateful, selfish person when you hear my story, but I have to take the chance that you might understand just a little. Please try not to judge me until you hear the whole story, and feel free to ask questions, but understand that I may not know the answers, that I might be asking myself the same questions."

In an effort to encourage and reassure Agatha, Greta reached over and patted her arm. "Just tell me your story, honey. I'm not in any position to judge. The Lord knows I've made enough mistakes in my own life. I just want to know the truth about you."

CHAPTER 5

What I remember about the last year I was at home in Kentucky is a little sketchy. My husband Seth was very busy. He was an insurance salesman for State Farm. He was out almost every night until eight or nine. The kids (ten and six)...I know it's strange, but I remember them as "the kids" not as individuals, Samuel and Abby. I'm not sure when I started thinking of them as "the kids" but I think it's significant because when they were younger I adored everything about them and noted their every unique quality. But somewhere along the way I lost touch with them. It wasn't healthy. Anyway, they were difficult in some ways. Samuel had a learning disability, some dyslexia, so he required a lot of help with homework, and Abby was very active and often did not behave in class. Being a teacher, I was probably bothered more by both these problems than I would have been otherwise. I remember dreading going home at night and being very frustrated with trying to help Samuel with his homework, which seemed so easy to me and so hard to him. But I did most of it without help from Seth. Seth seemed to think I babied Samuel too much and practically did his work for him. Maybe I did. I remember thinking that I was a very poor mother. I would get very angry at Abby when her teacher sent home notes about her behavior in school. In her case, Seth didn't seem to think it was any big thing and said I was too hard on her. As her name implied, Abigail's father "rejoiced in her."

"Just ignore it," he'd say. "The teacher is probably exaggerating anyway."

So here I was—too easy on one and too hard on the other. I couldn't seem to get it right.

I came to view Seth as someone who was unhappy with me. One night I had a very vivid dream. I can still remember it. Seth was yelling at me and telling me to stop saying something about one of the kids. However, when I looked into his face it was not Seth Johnson, but my father. I don't know why I remember it, but it was so real.

I may have tried to avoid dealing with the problems of my children by getting very involved in both school activities and teacher organizations. I taught eighth grade English and reading for about fifteen years and for the most part enjoyed my teaching. I taught school in a rural area of Southeastern Kentucky not far from where I grew up. It was called Royal Oaks School and was a consolidation of several one and two-room schools in the area. My maiden name was Royal, and I think the school was named for one of my relatives, but I never knew the story or why it was named that. In fact, I attended the school from fifth grade through eighth, and some of my former teachers were still there. I became very active in the Kentucky Education Association (KEA) and gained satisfaction from that. I felt I was drifting away from my family and more into my work. I enjoyed my work and teacher organizations and dreaded being at home.

Despite that, however, my work and KEA activities put a lot of pressure on me. By the end of the school year, I was looking forward to being out of school. I thought the fact that the kids would have no homework and no opportunities to misbehave at school would be wonderful. We did not have big plans for the summer—no vacation trips to the beach or anything like that. I scheduled the kids for several weeks of camp, but *on the days that they were home, they complained because they were "bored" and I was too hard on them. Seth, busy as always, had no time for us, and he went to several insurance meetings that summer. I was scheduled to go to a KEA conference for four days the week before the opening of school, and as it turned out, I looked forward to that the whole summer.*

Now that I look back on it, I was probably depressed for at least a year, maybe longer, before that fall. But at the time, it just seemed that my life was miserable. I had no one to talk to about it. Seth is a good man, but he is not one who would understand someone's feelings. I have wondered what he would have said had I told him how I felt. I still do not believe he would have made much effort to understand. He just seemed to think people should go ahead and do what they need to do and not complain or talk about it. I remember once trying to tell him that I felt like I was not a very good mother. I needed him to tell me that I was a good mother. What he said was that I could be if I would just stop worrying about it and do it! I don't know what he meant by that exactly, but what I heard was, "No you're not, but you could be."

I had friends at school, but they were "professional" friends. I might have talked to them about problems with a student, the principal, or even another teacher, but never about personal feelings. Actually, I felt that my teacher friends generally looked up to me as a leader. The other seventh and eighth grade teachers were relatively new and they would often ask my help and opinion in solving their own problems. I guess I felt that I could not let my guard down.

In August, I began to feel a lot of stress about beginning the new school year. It was not so much about the teaching itself, but about all the other responsibilities, especially those at home. I thought the KEA conference would be a great experience, and it was, but by the time it was over, I was even more stressed at the idea of getting back to my school routine. By the time the first day of pre-planning rolled around, I had to drag myself up and to school. When I got there, I was greeted warmly by the other teachers, and was given congratulations because I had been elected president of our local KEA organization for that school year. I remember wishing I could be happy about that, but being only burdened by it.

Both my kids attended the school where I taught. Sometime that morning I stopped by the office to see who their teachers were. Unfortunately, I did not feel good about either of their teachers. Samuel's teacher was one who had a reputation for not being good with kids who had learning problems, and Abby's teacher was very strict. I could see what my year at home would be like. I did mention this to a teacher friend, but she said she was sure they'd be fine—she had no children, so she did not have much to go on.

We had four days of pre-planning. Day two went okay, with several teacher meetings and the rest of the time spent on getting our rooms ready, and in my case taking calls for KEA problems. By the third day, I still had not done much actual lesson planning, and had only one bulletin board up. I worked hard all day, and made some progress. I went home exhausted, and immediately got to work cooking dinner. My friend's daughter Sherri, who had been staying with the kids, entertained them well but never did anything to clean up after them or make them clean up their messes, so things were pretty much a wreck. I was angry and tired. I ordered the kids to pick up their toys, dishes, blankets, and all the other clutter. They just ran upstairs laughing, as if I were joking. I was about to follow them, then decided against it. Instead, I picked it up myself, hating my life and my role. I felt that I had no control. That night I spoke with Seth about it and he just said I took things too seriously, but he did promise to talk to the Samuel and Abby about picking up their things tomorrow. I want to explain that Seth is not a bad person, or an uncaring one. He just did not know what I was going through. He could not hear it. I don't know how to explain it, but I don't want you to think I'm blaming my behavior on him. It's just the way it was.

Three incidents are crucial in my decision to do what I did. None of the three actually caused my actions, and none of them could have been predicted, but the memory of them makes them important events in my last days at home. The first was a news broadcast on Monday evening after dinner. I remember the newscaster's words were "What happened to Whitney Carruso?" What followed was a story of a woman who had just disappeared without a trace two years before. Foul play was not suspected because of the circumstances (I don't remember what they were), but her family was still looking for her. I remember thinking about that story for several days, wondering how she did that and what her reasons were. Somehow, I identified with her.

The second event was a comment made by a colleague in a brief conversation about the stress of starting a new school year. She said, "I don't know why I get so stressed out at the beginning of school. You know, you think everything is so important, but sometimes I wonder if anyone would even notice if I just didn't show up. I feel like I'm such a small cog in the big wheel." In my state of mind, I kept replaying her words the rest of the week. That was exactly the way I felt—nobody really noticed me.

As I thought about the woman who had disappeared, and as I reflected on what this teacher had said, I guess I was planning an "escape" even when I would not have admitted to myself or anyone else that I was doing so. I remember going to buy a wig at a beauty shop downtown. I told the woman that I needed one in case I got up one morning and didn't have time to do my hair before school. She watched me as I selected a wig that was exactly the opposite from my real hair and said, "Boy, will the students be surprised on those days!"

I replied, "Well, it'll give them something to talk about." I could see the shock in their eyes as they would see me in the hall or classroom. Other things I did that week now appear as planning for my departure. I did not see them as such then. I know it's crazy, but it's true.

I made it through pre-planning days, and by five on Friday, I had my room ready for Monday. As for lesson plans, I left the school laden with books and everything I needed to plan at home. When I entered the door, I noticed it was quiet, which probably meant the kids were out playing on the street with friends and Seth was working late—again. As I was about to turn around and go back to the porch to look for Abby, I heard a noise from the living room and realized that Sherri and her boyfriend were in there. Lately this had happened several times, and I was not happy with this development, but had not said much to her about it. I guess they had heard me and stopped whatever they were doing—I did not even dare speculate. Anyway, she came out straightening her clothes and hair and confirmed the fact that the kids were not in the house. They were next door playing with friends. As usual, she had not used the time they were out to pick up the "litter" scattered around the house. I did not have the energy to confront her. I thanked her and told her I would see her on Monday. For some reason, I felt as if I were lying to her, but at the time I didn't know why.

After Sherri left, I walked upstairs as if in a trance. I glanced around my room and then opened my closet door where my eyes were immediately drawn to a small suitcase I had never used. A friend had left one with me when she moved into a small apartment. Now, without thinking, I pulled the small case out and opened it on my bed. Why am I doing this? I thought. I immediately opened the drawer where I'd stored (hidden) the wig I had bought a few days before and put it into the case. Then I pulled a few other things from a drawer and put them in the case. I remember actually thinking, what am I doing? I'm not going anywhere. But here I was, packing a suitcase. Quickly, I closed the case and put it back in the closet. I felt almost as if I were watching myself as I did these things. I honestly can't say that I was thinking ahead at all. I was just going through the motions without much thought. A few minutes later I heard the kids come in downstairs. I didn't want to see them. I felt guilty, as if I'd done something I didn't want them to know about.

I don't remember much about that evening, except that Seth came in rather late and complained about dinner being cold, so I must have fixed dinner, but I don't actually remember eating. During the previous weeks, I would often put their dinner on the table, call them to eat, and then go into the den and watch the news or read the paper while they ate. That may be what I did that night. I also remember that the kids were in bed (or at least in their rooms) when Seth got home. I remember going to bed feeling very tired and overwhelmed with life.

I overslept Saturday morning and when I woke up, Seth and the kids had already had breakfast and were gone. A note on the table said something about an early baseball meeting or practice and a reminder that Seth had no clean white shirts for next week. For some reason, the note left me feeling as if I were being criticized both for oversleeping and for not having done laundry.

I ran upstairs, grabbed the laundry basket with the shirts and a few other things and went to the washing machine. I dumped all the clothes in the washer, put in some detergent, and turned on the hot water. Before I could close the door on the washer, I noticed that something wasn't right; the water coming out of the opening looked funny. By the time I realized what was wrong, the washing machine had dumped at least a gallon of reddish brown water all over the white shirts. I know this sounds crazy, but I felt as if I had experienced something like this before. As I stood in the laundry room, I felt like a small child. All of a sudden I felt panicky. My heart was racing and my hands were shaking. (My counselor attached a lot of significance to my feelings about this, but I'll save that for later.) Anyway, I turned off the water, came out of the laundry room, and closed the door as if to hide my dirty deed. I looked at the clock and back at the note on the table, and suddenly I felt that I had to get out before Seth got back. I only had about forty-five minutes to "escape." I ran upstairs, got the little suitcase I had packed, added some of my make-up and other toiletries. Then I looked into a drawer where I had a few hundred dollars in cash which I had earned tutoring our neighbor's son in reading that summer. I tucked it into a side pocket of the suitcase, and in about fifteen minutes, I was in my car and on the road going somewhere. I headed south and just kept driving until I got to Knoxville. When I saw the sign to Nashville via I-40, I took the exit and continued until I reached Nashville. During all that time, I don't remember ever asking myself what the heck I thought I was doing. I just drove. Sometime in the afternoon, I checked into a motel. On Monday, I asked the clerk if he knew where I might find a job and he recommended a few restaurants. The rest you know.

CHAPTER 6

During Agatha's story, Greta had gradually moved toward the edge of the sofa, wide-eyed, occasionally shifting her weight from one side to the other or starting to interrupt, but deciding to let Agatha continue. When the story was finished, she arose and stared at her friend.

"Wow! I just don't know what to say. I had no idea. You seemed—seem—so normal, so well adjusted. Why do you think all this happened? Did you just become depressed?" She walked over and sat closer to Agatha. "Has the counselor helped you to understand things better? What did you mean about the counselor's comment about the significance of your feelings about the incident in the laundry room?"

"Well, about the depression. Yes, I think I had become more depressed than I realized. No, I still don't really understand exactly what happened to me, or why it happened." Agatha looked helpless as she gazed into her cup of coffee. "That's one reason I'm so scared to go back."

"So why did the counselor think the laundry incident was important?"

"I'm not sure. He just started asking me about my childhood, and that's when I sort of backed off. I really have never been able to talk much about when I was young. I just really don't remember much about my life as a child."

"You said you had a dream about Seth being mad at you, but it was your father's face. Was your dad abusive or something?"

"No. No, I didn't even live with my father. I lived with my grandmother," said Katie.

"Did you know your father? Maybe you were traumatized because you had no parents," said Greta musingly.

"I don't think so. I knew my dad. He lived next door with Liz, his second wife, so I saw him often. My mother left when I was a baby and dad remarried a couple of years later. I never heard from my mother again."

"What happened to her?" asked Greta.

"I really don't know. I got the impression she just was not ready for the responsibility of a baby and just couldn't deal with it."

"But wouldn't she have come back later?"

"Greta, I just don't know. I guess I just never thought about it that much. My grandmother was a good mother to me, and I was happy."

"Did you ever stay with your father? Maybe you stayed with him and either he or your stepmother was mean to you," said Greta.

"No, you don't understand. I never stayed with them. Although they lived nearby, my grandmother raised me, and I never went over there. I don't even remember going over there during the daytime, although I might have. But my dad and stepmother came over to grandmother's a lot, so I saw him regularly, and anyway, he was a very gentle person. Neither he nor Liz ever spoke an unkind word to me," Katie said. "I really hardly remember *anyone* speaking an unkind word to me. That's what's so weird, so hard to understand. I just don't know what happened to me, but I really dread facing my family and my neighbors again. I don't know if I can do it. Maybe I'm just not ready yet."

"But don't you miss your children and want to be with them? I mean, I don't have children, but I always thought that mothers had this bond with their children," said Greta.

"That's the funny thing. I feel like I ought to miss them and want to go back, but I really don't, at least most of the time I don't. Occasionally I miss seeing them and at those times, I would give my life to be with them, but then I seem to shut my mind to them and just almost forget they exist. It's really strange, I know. I've talked to the counselor a little about this, but he seems to think that once I fully recover from the depression, I'll gradually get back to my former self."

"So he thinks it's all a part of the depression?" asked Greta.

"Well, he just says that sometimes when we get depressed, we have to shut out concern for others in order to survive for a while. And he says that even when I go back it may take a while to re-connect with my family. He says I may have to just act the part until the feelings come back. That kind of scares me."

Greta shifted in her chair, seeming a little uncomfortable, and then asked, "Have you told Kirk anything about all this?"

Agatha looked panicky. "No, of course not. Well, I mean I did mention to him that I might have to leave Nashville and go back to see my family. Why?"

"Well, the last time I saw him, he acted kind of strange. I think he really likes you, not just as a friend, but more than that. And, well, he…he just seemed kind of weird when he mentioned you."

"When was that?" asked Agatha.

"Yesterday."

"Yesterday? What did he say?" Agatha's face registered her anxiety. "I talked to him this morning and he never mentioned talking to you."

"Well, he came into the restaurant and started asking me about our trip to the park. He wanted to know what we were talking about. He seemed almost to be accusing me of something, but I couldn't figure out what I had done, so I just finally told him I had to get back to my customers and he left."

"Oh, that makes me *so* angry," said Agatha, seething. "What right does he have to follow me around and question my friends about me? I've told him I have no interest in a relationship with anyone right now."

"Well, obviously he didn't get that. He seems a little weird, don't you think?"

"Well, when I first met him he seemed really nice, and I guess not knowing many people here, I sort of encouraged him, and considered him a friend. But lately, yes, he's beginning to seem a bit strange," said Agatha. "I just don't know what to do. I think I'll have to talk to him about coming and talking to you at work. That's just crossing the line as far as I'm concerned."

"He may be mad at me for telling you, but I just thought you should know," said Greta, looking a little worried. "Are you going to call him or what?"

"I don't know. I'll have to think about it."

It was nearly midnight that night when Greta left, so Agatha thought she'd try to forget about Kirk until the next morning. She watched from the window as Greta backed out of the driveway, then straightened up the living room a little and decided to make a cup of hot chocolate before going to bed. As she walked into the kitchen, the phone rang. When she answered, for some reason she was not surprised to hear Kirk's voice at the other end of the line.

"You're up late," he said. "Must've had late company or something."

"Kirk, what's wrong with you?" Agatha almost shouted. "Why are you acting this way? You know it's none of your business what I do or who I have over! Have you gone crazy or something?"

"Hey, calm down. I just thought since you were up, you might want to talk," Kirk said. Agatha could almost see a sneer on his face.

"How did you know I was up? Are you watching my house or something?"

"Well, let's just say, I saw Greta's car leave about five minutes ago, as I happened to be driving by your house," Kirk said, with a little laugh.

"That's against the law, you know," said Agatha.

"What, driving through your neighborhood, or calling you at midnight?" he said smugly. "I often drive through Berry Hill on my way home from the grocery store."

By this time Agatha felt really angry, but also a bit panicky. She knew that what he had done was not really criminal, but she feared that it might become that if he kept it up. How had Kirk turned so ugly so quickly? Why hadn't she seen it coming? Maybe she hadn't wanted to see it. In a way, she realized she had used Kirk by not telling him the truth about herself. How was he supposed to know she was married if she did not tell him? For her part, she knew she could not get involved with anyone because she was married, but Kirk had no way of knowing that. So they were looking at the relationship from totally different perspectives, and that was her fault. But still, if she wasn't interested in a romantic relationship, no matter what the reason, he should respect that.

"So, which is it that's a crime?" Kirk said, pressing for an answer.

"Well, I guess it's not a crime, but if you keep it up, it could be considered stalking," Agatha answered.

"Tell you what, go to dinner with me tomorrow night, and I'll promise to stay within the law," he said.

"I'll go to dinner with you because we need to talk and come to an understanding about some things, but please don't consider this a date, Kirk, because it isn't," Agatha said.

"Okay, I'll take that I guess if that's what you want. Pick you up at seven," he said.

"All right, see you then," Agatha said resignedly. She could think of nothing she wanted to do less than go to dinner with Kirk, but she did need to talk to him, and end the relationship once and for all.

When Kirk picked her up the next evening, however, she could tell that the thought of ending the relationship was the farthest thing from his mind. He showed up with flowers, a big smile, and a hug for her. When they were in the car, he told her that they were going to the most romantic restaurant in Nashville. Obviously, he had either refused to hear what she had said or had forgotten all about it.

As soon as they entered the restaurant, he made it plain that he had reservations, and when they were seated, he ordered an expensive wine which she suspected he could not afford.

"Kirk, why are you doing this? Didn't you listen to a word I said last night?" Agatha said, hating to have to bring it up, yet knowing she had to get it out in the open.

"Oh, Agatha, all couples have fights. The fun part is making up. You know I only talked to Greta because I care about you, and last night, I just wondered what you were doing and maybe I got a little carried away. I won't do it again, I promise. Just say everything's all right and it will be."

"No! Everything is NOT all right. First of all, I'm not ready for a relationship with anyone right now, so it's nothing personal, but you've got to listen to me when I tell you that we cannot go on like this, you trying to get into a romantic relationship and me telling you that I'm not interested. Also, it's more than just one or two incidences. You seem to think you own me all of a sudden or something. Just back off! Don't you understand?" Agatha realized she was nearly shouting and some people at a table near them were staring.

She could tell by the look on Kirk's face that he was very upset, and she couldn't tell whether it was anger, hurt, embarrassment, or what. Finally he took a deep breath, and said (amazingly), "Maybe we just need to start over...let's just pretend that we just walked in—and we'll just order our dinner and talk about something else."

What could she say? "Okay, I guess that's the best thing to do, under the circumstances," she said.

"So, have you ever eaten here before?" he asked, as if they had just walked in.

"Only once, and that was right after I came to Nashville," she said.

"Well, I really like their salmon," he said. "But you order whatever you want."

The rest of the evening was like that, polite conversation. Agatha didn't know what to do. On the one hand, her only purpose for coming out with Kirk was to tell him that he should not count on a romantic relationship with her, that he *could* not. But on the other hand, she really did not want to get into another shouting match with him over it. By the end of the meal, she was feeling very awkward. She knew that the right thing would be to tell him the truth, that she was married and that she was not who he thought she was. Somehow she feared telling him. She had this strange feeling that bad things would happen if she told him. Finally she decided to try to buy some time in a way that would not make him angry, but might keep him from harassing her.

"Kirk, I'm sorry if I've hurt you lately. I know that I've been avoiding you and you don't deserve to be shunned. But I really need some time to work out some of my own issues. Can you understand that?"

"Can I understand that? Can I understand that? What do you think I am? An idiot? Of course I understand it. You don't want to see me. You don't want to talk to me. You want me to leave you alone. I've understood all of that all along. But what *you* don't seem to understand is that you don't lead someone along and act like you care for them and then all of a sudden just drop them, like a piece of china. It breaks you know, it shatters. And so does a person. So you can't do that. It's not right."

Agatha realized then that there was no reasoning with this guy. He wasn't thinking logically. She was trapped in his unreasonable cycle of thinking and no matter what she said, it would be wrong, but she had to keep trying.

"Kirk," she said trying to speak kindly. "Have I ever said anything to you to indicate that I was interested in a relationship with you other than just friendship? Have I ever mentioned marriage, a future, ever dressed provocatively, or suggested in any way that I wanted a romantic relationship?"

"Of course you have," he said forcefully. "Women like you will never admit it, but they lead a fellow on and then say they didn't mean to."

"Women like me?" Agatha asked weakly. "What do you mean?"

"You know what I mean," Kirk said adamantly. "You're a whore, just like most women I've known."

"Kirk," said Agatha in one last effort to get through to him. "If I've misled you, I'm sorry. But please understand that I'm not the kind of person you think I am. The first time you suggested that there was something more between us than friendship, I suggested that we stop seeing each other. That's because I did *not* want to lead you on into thinking there was something more." When she finished speaking, Agatha stood and said, "I think I should go now. I'll find my own way home."

Kirk was silent and did not attempt to stop her or follow her out of the restaurant, but she knew it was not really over as far as Kirk was concerned. She walked for a few blocks before she found a pay phone and called Greta to come and get her. By the time she heard the distinctive sound of Greta's beat-up red Ford coming down the street, Agatha was beginning to experience real fear of what the next few weeks would be like. Almost before Greta got to a complete stop, Agatha jumped in the front seat and slumped down.

"What's wrong?" said Greta. "You sounded as if you were scared to death or something."

"Could you just take me home, please," Agatha snapped.

"Hey, wait a minute," Greta retorted. "I'm just trying to help."

"Oh, I'm sorry, Greta. I know you are. I'm just so frustrated with Kirk. And you're right. I'm half scared. I think he's kind of crazy. I just don't know what to do. I can't get through to him. I kept telling him I was not interested in a romantic relationship, but he wouldn't listen. Now he accuses me of leading him on, but I don't think I did."

"I don't think you did either," said Greta sympathetically.

"But in a way I do feel guilty because I deceived everyone about who I am, so I blame myself for getting into this whole mess."

"Well, maybe now he'll just go away and leave you alone."

"I hope so," said Agatha, "but I'm not really convinced that he will after the way he talked today. He actually called me whore, and he also said I was 'like all the other women he'd known.' That sounds kind of sick to me." Greta did not respond and Agatha suspected she agreed that Kirk would probably not stop the harassment. When they arrived at Agatha's house, Greta offered to go in with her, but Agatha insisted that all she needed was a good night's rest and she would be fine.

The aroma of the cake she had baked earlier met her as she entered her house. She slipped off her shoes at the door and the cool hardwood floor felt good to her feet. She poured a glass of tea and cut a huge wedge of chocolate cake before sitting down in her favorite chair and turning on the television. As soon as she finished her cake and tea she settled back to watch the news before getting ready for bed. The long tense evening had exhausted her and she did not want to try to sort out all her problems. She decided to save that for tomorrow.

CHAPTER 7

For several days, she heard nothing from Kirk or from her husband Seth. She hoped that Kirk had just lost his temper and is now over it and has gone his own way. She threw herself into her work and tried to push her problems aside. She appreciated the fact that Seth had agreed to wait a few weeks and she could almost pretend that things were "normal." Unfortunately, that feeling did not last long.

About a week after she had left Kirk at the restaurant, she happened to look out her window one evening just before dark, and saw a black pick-up truck pull up and stop across the street. She thought nothing of it at first, but she noticed that whoever was driving did not get out of the truck. She wondered if the driver was there to pick up her neighbor's daughter, but usually her friends went inside, or at least went to the door. Agatha finished a load of laundry and then ironed the dress she needed for the next day. She remembered that she had left the book she had bought earlier in her car, so she went out to get it. It was dark now but the street lights gave plenty of light for her task. She picked up the book, pushed the lock on the car door down and started back in the house when she realized that the pick-up was still parked across the street. Immediately feeling uneasy, she quickly went inside and locked the door. When she got to where she could look out the window without being seen from the street, she peeked out to see the silhouette of a man in the truck. A few minutes later, the engine started and as he pulled out into the light of the street she could see it was Kirk!

Agatha felt the color drain from her face. She stood frozen beside the bathroom window where she had positioned herself in order to be able to see the street without being seen. Her first thoughts were questions. What was he doing there? Why would he come to her house and not come to the door? What should she do? Who could she call to ask what to do? After several minutes of standing there unable to move, she went back into the living room and picked up the phone. She dialed Greta's number. After three rings, Greta's cheerful voice came on the line.

"Hello!" she said.

"Hello, Greta," Agatha said cautiously.

"What's wrong?" Greta said, immediately recognizing the concern in Agatha's voice.

"I'm not sure, I mean... Well, Kirk's been sitting in a parked truck across from my house for over an hour this evening and..." Agatha stopped, not knowing what else to say.

"Is he still there?" Greta asked.

"No. He just left a few minutes ago."

"Did he say anything?"

"No, he just sat there. When he pulled out where the street light was on his face, I saw that it was Kirk."

"Are you sure? Could you have just imagined it to be him?"

"No," said Agatha, "I have no doubt that it was Kirk. He even had on a shirt that I recognized, but I saw his face plainly."

"Didn't you tell me that one time before, you had seen him driving by your place?"

"Yes, and he did not deny it, but more or less said he just 'happened to drive by' on his way to somewhere else, and that it was 'no crime.'"

"I call this stalking. You should tell the police," Greta said.

"Well, he didn't really do anything. Do you think they'd consider that a crime?" asked Agatha.

"Probably not, but they might pay more attention to you the next time in case he did bother you."

"I just don't know what to do. Maybe I should just call him and ask him not to be coming over here again," said Agatha.

"Huh," said Greta "Like that would do any good. He'll just get mad, that's all."

"You're probably right, but I just can't see myself calling the police on him."

"Well, do whatever you like, but I think he's a jerk, and he could be dangerous," observed Greta.

"I guess I'll just sleep on it. I appreciate your input though."

"Call any time," said her friend.

By the time Agatha got off the phone with Greta, her mind was in a turmoil. She had the distinct feeling that she was in some real trouble. Although she had tried to downplay the ramifications of what she had seen, she basically agreed with Greta. She went back over all the things Kirk had said and the anger he had expressed when she last talked to him. She went to bed, but she knew she would not sleep. She got out of bed several times to look out the window to see if anyone was there. Looking at the empty street, she finally decided to give him one more chance before calling the police. After all, he had not really done anything except sit there, and in the past he had really been a good friend to her. She got her book and turned on the light to read a while. Although her thoughts kept going back to her problem with Kirk, she did begin to feel sleepy and finally turned off the light at three o'clock and fell asleep.

She awoke to the ringing of the phone at 8:30 in the morning. Who could be calling at this hour? She grabbed the phone, hoping it might be Greta checking on her. The voice on the other end was familiar, but not Greta's.

"Well, hello, hope I didn't wake you," Kirk said amicably.

"Yes, as a matter of fact you did," said Agatha guardedly.

"I was just calling to check on you since you never call me these days. I just wanted to make sure you were all right, not having problems or anything."

"Actually, I had planned to call you today Kirk," said Agatha, trying to sound calm. "I was going to ask you to stop stalking me or I will have to call the police."

"I wasn't stalking you. It must have been your imagination. You probably wished I had come to see you."

"Believe me, I wasn't imagining that you were in that truck. And I certainly was not wishing you had come to see me," Agatha said, raising her voice for emphasis.

"But I don't own a truck. Gotcha there," he said smugly.

"I don't know who owns the truck. All I know is that you were in it."

"Can you prove it?" asked Kirk.

"I witnessed it," she shot back.

"So it's my word against yours then," he said.

The conversation was going nowhere. Agatha shifted in her chair and gave it one last shot. "Kirk, I know you were in front of my house last night, and I know you are calling me this morning just to see if I knew it, so don't try to deny it. Let's just put it this way. If you show up here again and/or keep calling me, I will call the police and get a restraining order against you."

"The police have rules you know; you can't just get restraining orders against people unless it's really legitimate. Just sitting in your vehicle on a street is not against the law."

"Well, it might be if you are stalking someone," she said.

"Whatever…I guess I'll see you around," he said, and hung up.

Agatha slammed the phone down! How dare he call her just to see if she had seen him. It was all a game to him. He thought he would just do enough to annoy her, but stay within the law. Well, she'd show him what was and was not lawful. She could hardly wait to catch him there again and call the police!

The next day was a busy one at work. It was nearly dark by the time she pulled into her driveway, and she automatically looked around to see if there were any cars on the street or anyone lurking around her house. She saw nothing. Unloading the car of the perishable items, she left the rest in the car and went inside. After putting the refrigerated items away, she proceeded to put other items in the pantry and bathroom, and then out of habit walked to the bathroom window and looked out. To her astonishment, she saw Kirk looking into her car window! Keep calm, she told herself. Go to the phone and call the police. She walked directly to the adjoining bedroom where she picked up the phone and dialed. After two rings, the phone was answered by a local policewoman and Agatha explained her problem. She was told that although she would have to come to the station on Monday to file a complaint and get a restraining order, they would send a patrolman down her street immediately and if he were still there, they would question his presence. Sure enough, in a few minutes Agatha saw a policeman drive by the house. By that time, however, Kirk was in his car, so they did not stop.

Soon she saw Kirk's car leave. About thirty minutes later, Agatha's phone rang and she was not surprised to hear Kirk's voice on the other end of the line.

"Whores like to tease and lead men on and then call the police," was all he said.

Agatha hung up the phone and went back into the living room. She quickly went out to her car, retrieved the items she had bought and then practically ran back into the house, where she locked the door securely and then pulled down all her blinds.

True to her plan, Agatha went to the police station on Monday morning and got a restraining order against Kirk. She knew he would basically ignore it, but at least she would have something on record in case she had to call them again.

The rest of the week she looked for any unusual activity around her house, but she saw nothing. On Saturday Seth was supposed to come, so she was trying to keep the weekend free so they could visit. She had given him directions to her house and decided to talk to him there. He had made reservations at a nearby motel for his late Friday night arrival. She had felt the need to have her little abode clean and neat and she had run several errands after getting off from work at three o'clock. The grocery store was her last stop, where she purchased items to make lunch for them on Saturday and some ice cream and cookies for a snack. Although she was nervous about seeing Seth, she was actually looking forward to it in a weird kind of way.

CHAPTER 8

The sun was shining when Agatha awoke Saturday morning. She immediately remembered that Seth would be coming over at ten o'clock and it was already almost nine. Despite the fact that she was a little anxious about seeing Seth, after her encounters with Kirk, it felt safe to have Seth coming to visit. She realized that *safe* was a good word in describing Seth. She had known him for so long, and she had never felt *unsafe* with him. But somehow that was what had driven her away, she *had felt unsafe* just before she left. There was a mystery there, and she was not sure it really had anything to do with Seth. She'd have to sort that out later, but right now she needed to jump in the shower and get ready for his visit.

Promptly at ten o'clock she saw the familiar dark green Chevrolet drive up in front of her house, and Seth opened the door and unwound his six-foot-two frame into a standing position. His face looked a little older, and his wavy black hair looked liked it might be needing a cut. She had always had to remind him to get an appointment. He looked around, seeming a little unsure of himself, and then walked up her sidewalk. She swallowed the giant lump in her throat, told her heart to stop pounding, and opened the door before he rang the bell. All the time she was thinking, what will we do—hug? Shake hands? Before she could answer the questions that loomed in front of her, Seth embraced her in a huge hug and they both started crying. Neither of them had really anticipated that. It just happened. In a few moments, they separated, stepped back and looked at one another. His face showed the wear and tear that her absence had caused.

"Well, I had not intended…I mean I…maybe I shouldn't have done that…I have gone over and over what I would say when I finally saw you, and well, I just don't know…" he stopped, and she saw that there was some anger in his face that she had expected, but had hoped would not be there.

"I know," she said. "It's the same with me. I mean, not the same, but I did not know how we would react. Well, you look good. Are you okay?"

"I'm fine," he said without emotion.

"And the kids, how're they? Do they know you're here?"

"Yes, to both questions," he said.

"Do they want to see me? What do they think?"

"Well, it's complicated, Katie. It's been really hard on them, not knowing where you were or what was going on. Actually Abby begged to come with me, but Samuel has been very quiet and expressed no interest in the whole thing."

Agatha was goaded into reality when Seth called her "Katie" and she had been used to being called "Agatha" for the last two years. She realized what a difficult situation she had caused, both here and in her hometown back in Kentucky. She also realized that maybe Seth didn't even want her to come home.

He certainly would be within his rights not to want her back. After a few moments of silence, Seth stood.

"I've got some things in the car I brought to show you. I'll be right back."

He brought a small briefcase, which he opened and pulled out a folder. When he opened it she saw that it contained several items, among them some newspaper clippings.

"I want to show you these, because it may help you to see what people were thinking back home after you left. I don't know if you ever really thought about that, and I really don't know where to start in terms of asking you what you were thinking. I just thought you needed to know what happened at home."

He carefully lifted one of the clippings, which looked as though it had been handled over and over. She could picture small hands clutching it and asking, "Where's Mommy?" She reached for it slowly, wondering whether she wanted to read it. It was a two-column article, with the title, "Teacher Reported Missing." At the top right was a one column picture of her, taken at school the year before she left. The article basically said that police were searching for her body in the river nearby, but so far nothing had been found. She had never even considered that they thought she'd died. As she looked through the clippings she realized that it was almost a week before the police (and Seth) had concluded that she had merely left, and even then they never learned how or in what direction she had gone. One of the articles mentioned that they had concluded that she had left on her own because the car was missing, and her suitcase and some other items were missing from her home. As she proceeded to look at the clippings, she was at first stunned and the color drained from her face. Then as she thought about how Seth and the kids must have felt, she was moved to tears, silent tears though. She didn't sob, not yet. She just sat there, wordless and silent.

"How could I have done this?" she said aloud.

"You're asking me?" Seth said, angrily. "I've gone over and over this, Katie, and I just can't figure how a mother can go off and leave her two babies without a word of explanation. At first of course I thought that you had to be sick or even dead to do that. After the police concluded that you had probably gone off intentionally, even though I could not argue with them, I really did not believe it. I still thought that someday I'd learn the truth and there'd be something to explain it—but there isn't, is there? You just left!" He rose from the couch, placing the clippings back in the folder. "You can have these. Most of what's in here is speculation anyway. I've practically memorized them though, so I don't need them," he said, handing them to her. He looked sad, as if he had just lost whatever hope he'd had.

He continued to stand, and after a moment, he spoke. "I have to ask you this Katie. Is there someone else? Or was there at the time you left? There has to be something."

She looked at him. "No, Seth. There is not, and has never been anyone else."

Oddly enough, she felt that he believed her, although he still seemed angry.

She walked around the room for a moment saying nothing. "Do you want a coke or something? I've got coffee still in the pot, too, if you want a cup."

"Yeah, I guess. Coffee'd be fine," he said. "And then I'd better be going."

"Seth, don't go. Not yet. We need to talk. I'm not sure where this is going, or even if you want me back, but I know that I don't want you to just walk away without any understanding of what happened to me."

"I don't even know what I want. I just know that until you called I had kept hoping that one day things would be clear to me and I could get you back and know what had driven you away. And then when you called I still hoped, stupid man that I am. But now, seeing you and talking to you, I just don't know."

"I'll get your coffee," Agatha said as she moved toward the kitchen. She returned with coffee for both of them and quickly returned to the kitchen for a plate of cookies. "Seth, I want you to know that I don't understand my actions too well myself, but I've been in counseling for several months now. That's the reason I finally got the courage to call home. I want you to know that I'm trying to answer that question too—how could I have done that? When I left it seemed like the only thing I could do, but after a while I realized that it wouldn't seem that way to anyone else, looking at my situation. And that's when I realized that I had to learn the answer. I will understand if you decide you don't want me back. I can even understand if you don't want me around the kids. I've betrayed them in a horrible way, and they may never forgive me. But regardless of what you decide, I've decided that I need go back and face whatever I ran away from. I don't think it was you or the kids."

"Are you saying that you want to come home?" Seth asked.

"I'm saying that I need to move back to Kentucky near home. If you want me back, given all I've done, I will come back home. But I don't want you to rush to a decision. You have a right to be angry and to not allow me to come back. I abdicated my rights when I walked out."

They talked a while about the kids' school and activities, about her work in Nashville, about the house she rented. Agatha felt like they were just getting to know one another in some ways. Seth had never talked much. She'd often wished he would talk to her more, but he had always preferred to watch television or read, and he had never seemed to think that what she had on her mind was interesting enough to talk about. Or at least that was the way she had felt. Today, though, he seemed to listen to what she said and it seemed as if an old friend had come to visit. They talked about some of the things they had done in the beginning of their marriage and even laughed a little. It was nearly twelve-thirty, when Agatha looked at the clock.

"Oh, I have stuff to make ham and Swiss cheese sandwiches for lunch. I have some potato salad too. Would you want to take them over to the Parthenon and eat?"

"Okay, sure. How long does it take to get there?"

"Not long. Fifteen to twenty minutes, depending on the traffic." In a few minutes she had the sandwiches made and the food all packed into a picnic basket and they were on their way, driving her car since she knew the way.

It was nearly four o'clock before they got back to her house and he was ready to leave. Over all, the visit had been positive for Agatha, but she was disappointed that he had never said whether he wanted her to come home. Although she certainly understood his feelings, she had hoped that at some point today he'd just say that of course he wanted her to come back. But as he started to leave, he never said it. He did, however, ask about returning for another visit.

"Would it be okay if I came back up toward the end of the month? Samuel has baseball games the next two weekends, so I know those are out, but maybe the last weekend."

"That will be fine," she said. In her mind she was contrasting his schedule which was tied to the kids and their activities with hers, which was basically open except for work. She was beginning to feel the impact of what was missing in her life. Soon he left, giving her a brief hug, but not saying anything.

After he left, she had the sinking feeling that when he returned, he would be telling her that he did not want her back in his life. It was a sad feeling, one which she had seldom had since knowing Seth. She kept asking herself what she could have said to make him more inclined to want her back. The sadness came from the knowledge that she really had no claim on him anymore. She had given him plenty reason not to want her back. After all, how could he trust her now?

CHAPTER 9

Agatha had spent Saturday night and most of Sunday sorting out all the thoughts about Seth's visit. She had read and reread the newspaper clippings, finding the reality of her actions disturbing. Before she really faced what she had done to her family, she had wondered only philosophically why she made the decision to leave. Now she was pained by the question. At work on Monday she kept thinking about the news clippings in her car. They were reality. They were taking her back to that weekend so many months ago. And nothing about it made sense any more. She had really walked out on her two young children, and she had lived the last two years as if they didn't exist. How *could* she have done that? *Why did she do it?*

"Excuse me, what?" she said, realizing that the customer was asking her for something.

"I just asked, *for the third time*, for some more coffee," said the irritated man.

"I'm so sorry, sir," apologized Agatha. "I was thinking about something else."

"Well, Missy, I would think your job would be to be thinking about what your customers need," he said sarcastically.

"Yes, sir. You're right. I'll get your coffee right away."

Agatha walked to the coffee area, shaking. I've got to get it together, she thought. This was the third time today that she had just completely tuned out everything around her, and a customer would almost be shouting at her. She wondered if any of them had reported her to her supervisor. She poured the coffee and made sure she paid close attention to the man's request for cream and sugar.

"Agatha, could you get table four, please." said her supervisor, "It's really in Kim's section, but she's really busy, and these people have been waiting for a few minutes."

As Agatha approached the table, she saw a couple and two young children, similar in age to Samuel and Abby. Her breath caught momentarily and she almost stopped before she reached the table. She stammered out her name and told them she would be their server. "What can I get you to drink?" she asked.

After a brief plea for cokes, both kids ordered milk and the parents ordered water. Agatha's head was spinning. She thought she might not be able to continue. She walked to the back and stopped for a moment.

"What's wrong? You look like you've seen a ghost," said Greta.

"I'm fine," lied Agatha. "I'm just a little out of breath from all this running around, trying to do my section and part of Kim's too. I'll be okay."

"Well, you really don't look well. And I overheard one of your customers saying you didn't even seem to hear her when she asked for some ketchup a few minutes ago," Greta answered. "It's just about an hour before this shift ends. Want to go to Starbucks for a cup of coffee?"

"Yes, that'd be great," said Agatha, relieved to realize the shift was that nearly finished. Maybe she could make it another hour without doing something really stupid.

"Here you are," she said pleasantly to the family with the little kids "Now what do you kids want to eat? "

"Hamburger with fries," said the older one. "Just plain—no mustard, ketchup or anything."

"Do you have hot dogs?" said the younger boy

"Of course. How would you like that? Mustard? Ketchup? Chili?"

"No, just plain," he said quietly. The parents ordered and Agatha felt strangely connected to the family, as if she already knew them. She put in their orders and made sure she delivered them as soon as they were ready.

"Wow! That was quick," said the mother. "You must have children of your own."

"I do. I have two, about the same ages as yours."

Agatha served another customer, and then went back to give the family their ticket. As she walked away, she felt as if she had seen her own children.

She practically ran to the restroom. Her face was white and beads of perspiration were forming on her forehead. She grabbed the sides of the sink and stood there shaking. Finally she regained control and walked out into the restaurant again.

Seeing Greta, she said, "Would you mind getting the money from that booth of Kim's? I don't feel so well."

"Sure, I'll get it," said Greta.

Agatha finished with her other customers and soon she and Greta were on their way out.   They drove separately to Starbucks.

"What was that all about?" asked Greta when they were seated."Did that family say something to insult you or something? They seemed very nice to me."

"Oh, they are," said Agatha. "It was just the kids. They reminded me of mine."

"Oh, I see," said Greta. "Did they look like your kids?"

"Yes, a little. But I was already pretty upset. I brought these to show you. Seth came Saturday, you know, and he brought these clippings from the local paper when I left. It's just made me realize what a terrible thing I did, and my mind's just been in a turmoil ever since."

"I wondered when you'd really get around to facing it. It seemed to me that you'd just blocked it out of your mind or something."

"I know. I thought I was dealing with it, but I really wasn't, was I? Somehow the newspaper clippings forced me to look at the reality. Here, look at them," said Agatha, pushing them toward Greta.

Greta stared at them for a long time, reading them over and over. "Yeah, I see what you mean," she finally said. "What did your husband say? How's he taking all of this?"

"Well, he's pretty angry, as he has a right to be. I don't know if he really wants me back. That's the bad part. We had a pretty good visit and we talked for a long time. I told him that I really didn't understand why I left, and that I understood if he didn't want me back. I told him he didn't need to make a decision then, but I guess I hoped he'd just say he wanted me back, but he didn't say that. In fact he didn't say anything. All he said was that he wanted to visit again at the end of the month. I don't know what that means. It may mean that he's trying to get the courage to tell me that he doesn't want me back."

"Well, what do you want? Do you want to go back?" asked Greta.

"I think so. I know I want to find out what really happened to me. Sometimes I feel like I must have just gone crazy. For the first few months I never even questioned why I left. I felt like it was the only thing to do. But as I talked with the counselor, I became more and more convinced that there was something missing, something I had not considered. Now I feel sure that there was some reason, some fear, and it had to come from somewhere—maybe in my childhood, I just don't know. But I think I'll have to go back and face it. The problem is that if Seth doesn't want me back in his life, I'm not sure where I'd go."

Greta sighed. "Well, I believe you'll work it all out eventually. But I'll really miss you. By the way, what have you heard from Kirk? Have you told him anything?"

"Oh, I hadn't told you, had I? I actually had a restraining order taken out against him last week."

"You what? What did he do?" Greta said, looking surprised.

"Well, he just kept showing up in front of my house and sitting in his car, and then one night he was outside, looking into my car in the driveway. So I called the police. He called me after that, sort of taunting me. I had to go down there last Monday and file a complaint. They said if he called me or came on my property, or even loitered across the street, to call them. Luckily I have not heard from him since. Maybe he's given up. At least I hope so."

"I hope so, too, but somehow I don't really believe he's given up," said Greta.

"I just haven't had time to think about it the last week, with Seth coming here and all. I probably wouldn't have seen him if he had been in my driveway."

"Did you tell Seth about Kirk?" asked Greta.

"No. Why? What could I tell him? There's this crazy man who has the idea he's my boyfriend?"

"I don't know. I was just thinking that if either one of them learned about the other one, it might be trouble for you. Think about it, what if Kirk saw Seth at your house, or what if Seth saw Kirk talking to you? Wouldn't that be bad for you, either way, since both of them think you somehow belong to them?"

"Well, I *am* Seth's wife, and I guess if he thought I was dating or something, he would be mad, but Kirk has no hold on me, so it's really none of his business. He probably would be mad, though, but I don't expect they're ever going to meet. Eventually, I'll tell Seth about Kirk, when and if he takes me back. If he doesn't' want me to come back, it doesn't matter anyway."

"Okay, but I sort of think you might ought to tell Seth about Kirk, no matter what he decides, because I think Kirk could be dangerous."

"Well, maybe I'll tell him when he comes the next time. I don't want to discuss it on the phone though," said Agatha.

"That's probably a good idea," agreed Greta. "I guess I'd better get going. I've got some laundry to do before tomorrow, and I've got to stop by my mom's and see how she's doing. She has not been feeling well lately."

"I'm sorry. I didn't know. I hope I've not kept you too long."

"No. That's fine. I wanted an update anyway, and Mom doesn't like me to hover over her, even when she's sick. I just want to run by and check."

CHAPTER 10

The last Saturday morning in October was cloudy and cool, and Agatha awoke early with mixed feelings about the weekend. In some ways she looked forward to seeing Seth again, but she also dreaded what he would say. He had called only once since his first visit, and had spoken to her only a few minutes, and only to make arrangements for his visit this weekend. She feared that he had decided he could not trust her enough to take her back. While she understood his feelings, it made her sad. It was remarkable, even to her, that all those months she had barely thought of Seth or the kids, and now that was all she thought about. Seth had promised to bring the kids' recent school pictures and a few snapshots of their ballgames, and other activities. She had bought each of the kids' some little gifts, just to begin to reconnect with them. She had no idea how they would receive the gifts, but she had to start somewhere, and since Seth had not put them on the phone, she assumed that they did not want to talk to her.

Since Seth had said he would come over around ten again this time, she took her time drinking her coffee, eating some cereal, and then getting dressed. By the time he arrived, she had been just waiting, rearranging the kids' gifts, straightening the living room, and looking out the window. Once she saw a car drive slowly by, which she thought looked like Kirk's, but never got a look at the driver's face. Her heart pounded. What if he came by? What if he saw Seth's car there, and stopped? She remembered Greta's words and wished she had warned Seth about this man. She walked into the kitchen, lost in thought. When the doorbell rang, she jumped. She was relieved to see Seth's car in the driveway.

When she opened the door, Seth looked relaxed and rested, and smiled briefly as he entered the room. She saw that he had a folder of pictures from Kodak in his hand, and she immediately asked to see them. Seth pointed to each one, telling when it was taken and what happened on that day. He seemed to treasure everything the kids did, and it made Agatha wonder how much he had changed during her absence. He really did seem different, and she commented on it.

"Well, I guess when you left, I realized how poor a parent I had been," he said matter-of-factly. "So I tried to start paying attention to what the kids really needed."

Agatha remembered how she'd been irritated with him for being so absorbed in his work he had ignored the kids. But at least he'd stayed with them, she chided herself.

"I got the kids a few things," she said timidly. "I don't know what to do to communicate to them that I care. I know they probably think I don't care."

"Well…" Seth stopped. "I don't know what to say, Katie. Abby's excited and keeps asking to see you. Samuel, though, he's just clammed up. He won't even talk to me. I've tried to get him to open up a little and let me know what he's thinking, but he just won't. I left them with Mom this weekend. I thought maybe she could talk to him, but I don't know."

"I was wondering if you could bring them over to see me," Agatha said. "But I guess we have a lot of talking about things before you'd want to do that."

"Katie, I just need to hear you explain exactly what happened when you left. That last few weeks, I knew something was wrong in a way, but I just didn't know how to ask you about it. You seemed so different, so 'apart' from me, I guess. I remember thinking you were like a ghost in the house. You were there, but you were very quiet, and you would just move around in a really weird way. Did you feel that way too? Like you weren't really a part of the family anymore?"

"Yes, that was exactly the way I felt—disconnected, not a part of anything. The thing is, I just don't really know why. At the time, it seemed kind of logical. I kept thinking it was just my situation. And then the day before I left, I knew I had to leave. It was like something was pushing me forward. But the real mystery was on the day I left. Do you remember that the washing machine was messed up and dumped reddish-brown water on all the clothes?"

"Yeah, I had forgotten about that. In all my concern about where you were, I didn't even see it until a day or so after you left. Did you see that?"

"Yes, that's what really freaked me out!"

"The washing machine?"

"Yes. When I saw that, I had this idea that I would be punished, that I'd really goofed up. I remember imagining that you were going to beat me or something. I kept seeing you coming at me with something."

"That is really strange. You know I'd never do that," said Seth seeming shocked at the idea.

"I guess, but at the time, I thought it possible."

"I just find that hard to believe," said Seth. He looked out the window. "It's pouring the rain now. That poor guy is getting soaked."

"Who?" asked Agatha.

"I don't know. Some guy. Looked like he may have been walking in front of your house, and then when it started to rain, he was running toward his car, but he sure got soaked," Seth said, as Agatha came up behind him.

She had a sinking feeling she knew who it was, and sure enough, she saw Kirk slam his car door and drive off. She felt as if all the color had drained from her face, and she excused herself and went into the bathroom to compose herself before she returned to talk to Seth. He did not seem to notice anything wrong, so she did not make any explanation although she knew she probably should do so. It just seemed so awkward to mention another man to Seth. He was already disappointed in her enough. If she started telling him about Kirk, it might cause him to turn the other way.

"How are your folks?" she asked.

"They're fine. I have to tell you, though, that they are not happy about my coming over here. They know how hurt I was, and they say I'm just asking to be hurt again."

"Are you? I mean, have you decided to trust me again?" she asked tentatively.

"If you want to know the truth, I don't know yet, but I know that I want to continue to see you and see what happens.

I'm trying to keep an open mind, but there are a lot of people who are telling me I'm crazy for even considering it." Seth looked Agatha in the eye. "What about you? What are you thinking?"

"I don't want to hurt you again, I know that. I guess we should take it slow. I have a job here, and I don't have to move back right now. Why don't we just continue to see one another? Maybe I could even go to Kentucky for a visit sometime soon. I had an eye-opening experience at work this week. I served this family with two kids about Samuel and Abby's age. It really hit me how horrible it must have been for them. I don't understand how I could not have thought about that."

"I don't understand that either," he said. "Maybe whatever caused you to freak out like that was so powerful you couldn't think about anything else."

"It has come back gradually, just little things have made me see what I really did. The newspaper clippings had the biggest impact. When I read them, they made me see things in a whole new light," she said, looking sad.

"Tell me about your life here. I know you work in a restaurant. What's that like? Have you made any friends?" asked Seth.

"Well, my life here is much simpler than my life in Kentucky. That part I think has been good for me. I just go to work, do my job, and come home and read, watch television, or cook a little."

"What about friends?"

Greta knew this would be a good time to tell him about Kirk, but she hesitated. "Well there's this one girl at work, Greta. She and I have become good friends. I never told her who I was until after I called you. She thought my name was Agatha Kingsley, and that I moved here from Birmingham. I've gone by that name since I moved here."

"How did you get identification with that name on it?"

"Oh it was pretty easy. I met this guy when I checked into a hotel the first day, and he gave me the name of a place where I could get what was considered a "temporary" identification card. He thought I was running away from an abusive husband." Agatha looked down, feeling ashamed to let him know that she had told someone, even a stranger, that he was abusive.

"So what about other friends, neighbors?" he asked.

"Well, actually there is…" at that point the phone rang and Agatha, knowing it was probably Kirk, took it in the kitchen.

Curious to know why she left the room, where there was a phone in plain view, Seth walked to the phone and picked it up to see if it was working. However, just as he picked it up, he heard Agatha say, "Hello." He felt guilty, but his curiosity made him hold the phone.

"Well, well, well," said the voice on the other line. "It looks like you've got you a new boyfriend."

"Kirk, I asked you not to call here," Agatha said, sounding scared (or maybe embarrassed). "I also saw you in front of my house a while ago."

"I was just seeing where that car was from—Kentucky, huh? Your new boyfriend from Kentucky?" Seth was outraged by that time. He slammed down the phone, walked to the kitchen door and pushed it open.

He glared at Agatha and said, "I'm leaving!"

"Wait, no, don't leave," she cried, tears streaming down her face as she hung up the phone. "Please, Seth, you don't understand."

"Oh, I understand perfectly," he said. "Here I was thinking you were all alone, but no, you've had a boyfriend all the time. Did you come here with him? How long have you been seeing him? Does he normally live here with you?"

"No, no, it's not that way at all. He's, well, he was a friend for a while, that's all…"

"It didn't sound that way to me. It sounded like he was pretty familiar with you and maybe a little jealous. That doesn't sound like 'just a friend' to me. I'm leaving now and I don't intend to come back. I should have listened to the advice I've been getting from all my friends and family back home!" He stormed out the door and raced out of the driveway.

Forgetting about the police saying to call them if she saw him at her home or he called her, Agatha ran to her bedroom and threw herself on her bed, sobbing uncontrollably.

CHAPTER 11

Nearly twenty minutes passed before Agatha calmed herself enough to remember that she was supposed to call the police if Kirk bothered her again. She started to the kitchen when she heard a knock at the door. With a sickening feeling she remembered she had not locked the door when Seth left just as she saw the doorknob turn and Kirk walked in. His face was red and he strode in like a man with a purpose. She knew that his anger was out of control, even before he spoke.

"You women are all alike, just whores, all of you! I thought you were different, but you're not. Just like the rest of them! I think you just need a good beating, to knock some sense into you, not that it'll do any good, but at least you'll know what happens to people like you when they encounter men who will not put up with their ways."

Agatha's feet felt as if they were nailed to the floor as she listened to his words. She wanted to run, to yell. She swallowed hard but no words would come out.

By this time he was right in front of her, and he grabbed her by the shoulders and started to shake her. "What do you have to say for yourself? Nothing? Of course not. There is nothing to say," he practically shouted at her.

Finally, she started to move, and he held on to her arm, dragging her across the room as she begin to kick and scream.

He got her to the fireplace and grabbed the poker from its holder and started beating her with it, then slammed her down on the floor with the hand with which he had been holding her.

As she fell, her leg hit the side of the hearth, and she felt as if her leg were breaking. She had a strange feeling as if she had experienced this before. The realization shocked her. The last thing she saw was his fist coming at her face.

She awoke in a room that she recognized immediately as a hospital room. Greta was sitting by her side, crying silently. As Agatha's eyes adjusted to the bright lights, she moaned softly and Greta arose immediately and looked at her.

"Hey, it's about time you woke up," she said. Her eyes looked red as if she'd been crying. She pushed the button on Agatha's bed, and almost immediately the door opened.

"She's awake now," said Greta.

"Good." The nurse looked at Agatha. "Are you up to talking? The police are here asking to talk to you as soon as possible."

"Okay," said Agatha. "I'll talk to them."

It didn't take long for the police to verify who had attacked Agatha, especially since they had the restraint already in place, and Greta's word that he had been stalking her. As soon as they left, Agatha tried to assess what had really happened to her.

"I was sure your leg was broken, but it wasn't, but you have a huge cut and some bruises. Your arm is about as bad and you have some small fractures, one on your hand, and one of your toes, I think. And your eye is really black."

"Ouch," said Agatha. "It feels like every bone in my body is hurt."

"Looks like it too, honey," said Greta.

"What happened? How did you learn about it?" Agatha asked.

"Well, I called you after I thought Seth was probably gone. I thought it strange that you didn't answer, but I waited a while and called back. Still no answer. Finally I called your next door neighbor. She said that there were no lights on, but your car was in the driveway. I immediately became concerned, especially when she said that she had seen a dark blue Nissan in your driveway earlier in the afternoon. I knew you would not have gone anywhere with Kirk, so I asked Mrs. Stephenson if she had a key. She said yes, and when I got there I knocked on your door and then went to get her. When we first went in we didn't see you because of the couch and then I saw you lying on the floor. I almost fainted. Somehow I dialed 911 and we waited until the ambulance got here. That was the longest few minutes of my life. Mrs. Stephenson followed me here and stayed until the doctor said they had you all fixed up and that you'd just need to rest a while and get a little of the anesthesia out of your system before you'd wake up. I was still worried though until you woke up."

"Thank you, Greta. You're a good friend. You need to go on home, though, and get some rest."

"Are you sure you don't want me to stay with you? I will be glad to."

"No, I'm sure I'll just sleep tonight. Maybe you could bring some of my toiletries over tomorrow though. Did the doctor say anything about how long I'd be here?"

"No he didn't. I guess he'll tell you in the morning. It's almost morning now--11:50 P.M." said Greta.

"It's that late? Gee, how long have I been here?"

"I think we got here about 8:00 or 8:30, something like that. I don't know. I know that I first tried to call you around six, but I really don't remember the time when I finally went over there. Do you know when it happened—what time?"

"Everything is a blur—Seth was there, then Kirk called and Seth listened in on the call and got mad, then left; then I lay on the bed and cried, then I was going to call the police, but Kirk came in and started yelling at me and beating me, then I blacked out and woke up here."

"So, did you ever tell Seth about Kirk, about the restraint and all?"

"No. And he's gone for good now. He's not coming back. He thinks Kirk is my boyfriend. He even asked if I left with him to begin with. It's just a big mess and it'll never get straightened out now," Agatha finished dejectedly.

"We'll have to call Seth and get it straightened out, Agatha," said Greta.

"No! Don't you dare. I can't do that to him. He's had enough trouble from me," said Agatha. "I can't hurt him anymore. He's through with me anyway, and I can't blame him."

"But he should have the facts and base his response on that, not on something he thinks is true, but isn't. You've never really been untrue to him with Kirk or anyone, have you?"

"No, of course not."

"Well, then, he needs to know that," said Greta.

"Maybe, but I'm not going to burden him with all this. I got myself into this, even if I wasn't being unfaithful to him."

"I think you just need to go to sleep now. We'll talk tomorrow when you're feeling better," promised Greta, sensing that Agatha was getting too tired to reason things out tonight.

The next day when she brought Agatha's toiletries, Greta noticed that her friend seemed quiet and not herself. She learned that the doctor had said that they were concerned that there might be some internal injuries due to the beating and that she would have to stay several more days. Agatha was also terribly sore and her face was badly bruised, especially around the eye. Also the doctor was concerned about damage to the eye. Greta stayed with her most of the day and made some phone calls, including one to the restaurant, explaining that it might be a while before Agatha could return to work. Greta tried to get Agatha to let her call Seth before she went to work that night, but Agatha was still against it. Greta knew it was really not her business, and she didn't really know what Seth was like or what he thought had happened between Agatha and Kirk, but she believed that he should know the facts.

"I won't be able to come tomorrow until after work," Greta told Agatha as she prepared to leave. "But you know you can call me anytime."

"Oh, I know, I'll be fine," said Agatha, with more confidence than she felt.

Greta stopped. "Are you sure you don't want me to call Seth?"

"No, I can't let you call him. He's really mad at me. I didn't tell you all he said, but it's just over. I'm not certain he'd planned to take me back anyway, but now…"

Agatha stopped and her face looked dark and sad.

"I may stop by on my way to work in the morning, if I can get away in time," said Greta. "Call if you need me."

"Thanks, I really appreciate you staying with me so long. I'll just try to sleep a while now." When Greta closed the door, Agatha sighed. What would she do? How would she manage, with no one to help her? Greta would help, but she had to work. Despite the fact that she had told Greta emphatically not to call Seth, she really wished that he knew and wondered what he would do if he knew what had happened.

Greta was saddened by her friend's situation, and she just could not get the thought out of her mind that she should call Seth. She had found his number on the table beside the telephone at Agatha's house when she was waiting for the ambulance and had stuck it in her purse, just in case. Agatha didn't know she had it. When she got home, Greta pulled it out of her purse and stared at it. Within seconds she was dialing the number. A young boy's voice answered the phone. "Could I speak with Seth?" Greta asked.

"Sure. Just a minute," he said. "Dad!" Greta heard him call.

A few seconds later, a deeper voice answered. "Seth here," he said.

"Hello," Greta said, feeling insecure. "This is Greta Wilson. You don't know me, but I'm Agatha's friend."

"Who? You're whose friend?" said the puzzled voice.

"Oh, I mean I'm Katie's friend in Nashville," said Greta.

"Well, I don't know what you want, but I think I already know enough about Katie's friends in Nashville," Seth said in an irritated voice. "I suppose she's asked you to call, to explain her actions. But I'm really not interested in hearing any more lies."

The image of Agatha's face in the hospital gave Greta courage and she sounded almost angry as she said, "Well, I think it might not hurt you to listen to what I have to say. Maybe you don't know as much as you think you do."

Unexpectedly, Seth's voice became calmer, almost weary, as he said, "Okay, I guess you can say whatever it is you called to say."

"Well, to begin with, I just came from the hospital, and Agatha's been hurt pretty badly, and I thought you should know," said Greta.

"What? What happened? Was she in an accident? Will she be okay?" Seth seemed almost frantic, and Greta knew immediately that she had done the right thing in calling him.

"Yes, they do think she'll be okay. You need to know that Agatha did not ask me to call you. In fact, she told me specifically not to, and she does not know that I found your number and decided to call you anyway," explained Greta.

"Why? Why did she not want you to call?" asked Seth.

"Well, you may know better than I do, but she said that you were angry with her when you left."

"But what does that have to do with her accident?" he asked.

"Well, it wasn't exactly an accident," said Greta. "She was beat up."

"Beat up? Who did it? Why?"

"She said that you thought she had a boyfriend. Is that right?"

"Yes, I heard some guy acting as if he were her boyfriend, and it wasn't a stranger. She obviously knew him."

"That's true. She did know him. He befriended her not long after she arrived here. He helped her find things she needed and she had dinner with him a couple of times. But when he started acting like he wanted more than just friendship, she told him that she wasn't interested. I didn't know why at first, but later when I learned that she was not really Agatha and that she was married, I understood why she tried to separate herself from him."

"But, what does this have to do with someone beating her up?"

"Kirk, that's the guy's name, didn't accept her rejection of his advances, and had begun to stalk her. He would park his car across the street and sometimes come into her driveway and look into her car, stuff like that. Recently she had to take out a restraining order against him. I guess he must have driven by while you were there and seen your car or something, because after you left he came in and beat her up."

"Oh, now I remember, I actually saw someone looking at the back of my car. She acted kind of funny when I asked about it. Then when he left, it wasn't long before the phone call. But I never put it all together."

"Anyway, I just thought you should know that she was hurt, and also that she really had not been dating anyone. I know that all of this must be very difficult for you, but at least I think you should know the facts and not assume things about her that are not true," said Greta.

There was silence at the other end of the line so long that Greta thought maybe he had hung up or left the phone. Finally Seth said, "Why do you think she did not want you to call me?"

"She just said she had caused you enough grief, and that she thought you were through with her. She said that she just couldn't hurt you anymore. She said that she had got herself into this and she'd have to get herself out of it."

"Tell me about her injuries," Seth said.

Greta told him as much as she could of what the doctors had said and why she was still in the hospital.

"Is she still in danger? Would this guy come back?"

"I think the police have him now. They already had the restraining order on file, so even if he had not hurt her, he would still have been arrested for violation of the order. Since he actually attacked her, it'll be worse for him."

"I'll be over there day after tomorrow," he said. "And Greta, don't let her go home and be by herself until I get there. Okay?"

Greta promised him to look after Agatha until he got there. When she hung up, she knew she had done the right thing, but she still feared telling Agatha, since Agatha was set against her calling Seth.

Greta carefully avoided any mention of Seth the next evening, and Agatha did not mention him either. The following morning Greta had planned to stay with Agatha most of the morning because she was working in the evening and didn't go in until three o'clock. She arrived about ten o'clock that morning. She wasn't sure what time Seth would be there. Agatha seemed depressed and had not even fixed herself up at all that morning

"You want me to help you with your hair and makeup?" Greta asked.

"Oh, I don't know. I'm not planning to do any entertaining," she said, in an effort at humor.

"Well, you never know when someone could walk in," said Greta. "Just let me fix your hair, and help you get your make-up."

"Greta, are you trying to tell me something? Did some people at work tell you that they were coming?"

"No, no," said Greta. "No one said anything like that. I just thought it'd be good for you to get fixed up a little, just in case."

But Agatha could tell that Greta was hiding something, and she kept pushing. Finally, Greta decided she may as well confess.

"Well, actually someone is coming today, but I don't know when," she admitted.

"Who?"

"Seth," said Greta.

Agatha's face lit up for a moment, and then she began to cry. "I didn't want you to tell him," she said.

"I know," said Greta, "but he needed to know. And he needed to know the truth about Kirk. It wasn't fair to let him think Kirk was a boyfriend of yours. I know that what you did hurt Seth, but he needs the facts in order to decide whether the two of you can reconcile. He doesn't need a bunch of mixed-up information in the middle of it."

"I guess you're right. I just hated to bring more trouble to Seth—by the way, how did you get his number?"

When Greta told her about finding it by her phone the night she got hurt, Agatha said, "That seems like so long ago, doesn't it? It seems worlds away. I wish it would all go away. I'm so scared."

"That's one reason I called Seth. I know that Kirk is still in jail right now, but my guess is he won't be for long. He'll make bail. And I don't like the idea of you being at home by yourself."

Just then there was a soft knock on the door and Seth walked in. Greta noted the shock on his face when he saw Agatha. She introduced herself and then left them alone.

CHAPTER 12

Agatha looked at Seth as he stood speechless for a few moments after Greta left. Finally she said, "I'm sorry about all this Seth. I told Greta not to call you, but she found your number and called anyway. I'm glad you came though."

"Katie," he began, "I...I...I've been thinking all the way over here about how I deserted you when you were in danger. I feel really bad about that."

"You had no way of knowing," she said.

"Well, you would probably have told me if I had been a little more willing to listen. I just jumped to conclusions without even letting you explain. I remember how I heard you pleading with me to listen as I walked out the door, so self-righteous and angry."

"Actually, I could not have predicted what happened either. I was afraid but it was more of a vague, general fear of him."

"Where is he now?" Seth asked, drawing up a chair beside her bed and sitting down.

"According to Greta he's still in jail, but she predicts he'll probably be bailed out soon. I'm sort of scared about what he'll do when he gets out. I don't know what would make them think he wouldn't come after me again. You know he was under a restraining order when he came to my house before, so I don't think he'll stop just because he got caught." She watched Seth take all this in. She wanted him to say he wouldn't let anything happen to her, that he'd protect her at all costs. But he didn't, not then. He just sat there, processing what she'd told him.

Finally, he said, "I can stay a few days. I'll talk to the police and see what's going on, what they plan to do."

"Thanks, Seth. I really appreciate it." Just then the doctor came in and they went through the whole awkward conversation about who he was and the whole situation she was in.

After the doctor left, Agatha said, "Seth, I want to explain to you about this whole thing with Kirk."

"Okay, but before you start, I want you to know that I believe you when you say there was never a romantic relationship between the two of you. Greta explained all that to me."

"I know, but I still wanted you to know just what happened. To begin with, I met Kirk not long after I went to work in Nashville, and he seemed really helpful and nice. At first he did not even act interested in what I called dating. I guess I was just so naïve that I assumed he understood and believed me when I would say things like, 'I'm not interested in dating anyone,' and 'I appreciate your friendship, but that's all I want.'

"Later, when I saw that he was interested in more, I just tried to distance myself from him, thinking that he'd get the idea. I spent more time with my friends at work, and just basically tried to keep busy with other things. When he persisted, I tried to be kind but firm. It just seemed that the more I tried to pull away, the more he pursued me."

"Sounds like a nut case to me," interjected Seth.

"Yes, he is, as I finally learned," she said, putting her hand to the huge bruise on her face. "Even before that I realized as he kept 'stalking' me that his was not a natural interest. That's when I became concerned and afraid of him. But until I was in too deep to get out without getting hurt, I didn't really know what I was dealing with. I just wanted to explain all that so you'd understand that I didn't intentionally lead him on. He of course tries to make it sound like I did, but I really didn't."

"I believe you, Katie. I really do," said Seth, patting her hand. "I guess I need to get out of here and let you rest a while now."

"Yes, that pain medicine the nurse brought right before you came in is beginning to kick in," she said.

"I need to find a place to stay and get a bite to eat. What if I bring you some outside food for dinner tonight?"

"Oh, I'd love that," she said, and for the first time in days, she smiled a faint smile. "By the way, why don't you just stay at my place? It's empty and I guess it's a mess, but it's free."

"Are you sure you don't mind?" Seth asked. "I mean, I don't mind getting a motel room, but if it's okay, it would save me a few bucks."

"No, please, the keys to my house are in that drawer right there. Just take them. Do you know how to get there from here?" Her last words sounded tired and it was obvious she was getting sleepy.

"I'm not sure, but if I can't, we'll talk about it later. You need some rest. I'll get out and scout around for something to eat and maybe I'll be able to find the house," he said, opening the drawer and getting the keys. By the time he left, she was almost asleep. He stopped by the nurses' station on his way out and got directions to the address of her house and left the hospital.

Agatha slept soundly for a while, and then awoke with a start when a male nurse opened her door still talking to someone in the hall. She jumped and cried out, causing the nurse to jump back quickly, "What's wrong? Is something wrong?"

Shaking her head, she smiled. "No, "I'm just a little 'jumpy' I guess. I was sound asleep. I heard your voice, and immediately thought you were the guy that beat me up," she admitted.

"Wow, looks like he really did a number on you. It's understandable that you were frightened. I won't hurt you though," he reassured her.

"It's okay, I'm awake now. I'm still sleepy though."

"I'll just check these machines then, and let you get back to sleep."

As soon as he left, she began to doze again, but her sleep was troubled and full of dreams. She dreamed that Kirk was coming through the door with a poker and she was helpless to move. Then she thought that she was fighting him off and he was choking her. Next she was holding the door trying to keep him from entering.

"Katie, Katie, wake up! Are you all right?" Suddenly she looked up into the face of Seth, looking concerned. "What's wrong?" he asked.

"I was dreaming I guess. I was fighting off Kirk," she said, still looking scared.

"You don't need to worry about Kirk today. Today's Saturday and I talked to the police and they said he'd be in jail at least until Monday. So we'll just take it one day at a time."

She sat there thinking that it sounded like Kirk might get out on Monday and Seth's "few days" would probably be about up by then. What would she do? She didn't say anything though. Seth's presence felt reassuring and although he hadn't said so, she did not think that he would leave her in danger.

"Well, guess what I brought? Minnie Pearl's Fried Chicken!" He put the food on her table and began to open it up. "Oh, by the way, I had no trouble finding your house. I had a shower, changed clothes, and had a short nap, then went looking for food."

"This is great. Just what I needed, a definite contrast from hospital food. Did you get something to eat? I mean, for you to eat?"

"Yeah, I had not had lunch, so I 'pigged out' at the barbecue place. I knew you didn't care much for that, so I stopped on the way here and picked up the chicken."

"When you went to my house," Agatha hesitated, "…was the living room a big mess?"

"No, actually it wasn't, but I think Greta and your neighbor cleaned it up a bit, so it probably was when you left. It's okay now though, and everything is back in place," he assured her.

"Good," she said, drinking a sip of the sweet tea he had brought.

They chatted about inconsequential things for a few minutes while she ate, and then he said, "Katie, we need to talk about getting you home."

"Well, the doctor hasn't said for sure, but I think he might release me tomorrow," she said.

"No, I mean about you really coming home, back to Kentucky," he said uncertainly.

"Oh," she said, kind of shocked that he just all of a sudden brought it up. "Do you mean you want me back at *our* home? Have you decided to give me another chance?"

"Yes, I have," said Seth. "You know, I realize that I haven't been saying much about it, but I guess there was never that big a decision to make. I told you that my friends and family back home kind of advised against it, so I sort of acted like maybe there was some question about whether I wanted you back. But really there never was any question in my mind about wanting you back. And when I heard that you had been hurt, I just realized how important you are to me, so if you want to come home, I want you to."

"Seth," she said, her voice breaking, "I don't know what to say…I just kind of assumed that you did not intend to have me back. And I couldn't blame you. I realized that I needed you back in my life as soon as you walked in the door that day, but I didn't dare hope that you'd….and then when Kirk called that day when you were there, and you got so angry, I just knew it was all over." By this time she was sobbing.

Seth came over and took her in his arms and held her as she cried. Careful to avoid hurting her bruised face and arms, he gently patted her and reassured her that everything would be all right. She quieted after a while and looked at him.

"Seth, I don't know if I can do it or not. Just move back home, I mean. I want to, but I can't just go back as if I had never left. How can I do that? I have so many questions in my mind. I don't even know why I left. I tried to tell Greta about it one day. I told her all about what led up to my leaving, and she said still didn't understand why I left. And the bad part was that I realized that I didn't know either."

Seth moved to a chair at the foot of her bed. "Well, you've been in counseling here. And you got to the point where you wanted to contact your family and begin to sort it all out. Maybe we could get the counselor to recommend someone in our area to continue working with you there. Maybe you'll understand more as you go along."

"You'd be willing to do that?"

He sat forward in his chair. "Of course. I want to understand, too. Maybe it's my fault. Partially at least," he said.

"I guess at the time I left I did think you were to blame in some way, but the more I think about it, the more I think it is something else, maybe something that has nothing to do with you."

"Getting back to the matter of you coming home. Are you saying you'd like to get an apartment in town for a few weeks before actually moving back in with us? I guess we could do that if that..."

"No, I don't think so. That'd be expensive and unnecessary. I was just saying that it will be awkward, but I believe whenever I come, I should just move back in if that's what you want. How do you think the kids will take it?"

Seth looked down at the floor. "Well, I don't know. Abby will be fine, I think. Samuel, on the other hand, I don't know about him. He's kind of funny. It may take longer for him to adjust. I think it may be his age, or maybe it's just his personality. Anyway, he's been pretty angry and hard to deal with lately, especially since I've been coming over here. But I figure he'll get straightened out eventually. He's a good kid."

"This has been terribly hard for him, I'm sure," said Katie. "I don't know if I'll ever be able to forgive myself for walking out like that. I've been thinking about it a lot lately, and I think I owe it to both you and the kids to try to understand what may have caused me to do that and be sure I never do anything like that again."

Seth looked at her for a long time. She imagined that he had never really considered that she might do it again. And of course she had not really considered it either until she spoke the words. And what would keep her from it unless she understood the cause?

When he stood, she panicked, thinking he might have decided against having her back. But he moved toward her and looked her straight in the eyes. Katie, we take risks every day, and today, I need to risk that we can work things out. And what I don't want to risk is leaving you here with that maniac stalking you."

His protective attitude reassured her. "Did you talk to the police about what will happen?"

"As a matter of fact, I did," said Seth. "In fact, that was the reason I brought up the subject of you coming back home. I don't like the idea of that man getting out of jail and you being at home alone. I talked to the police about that. He said that his court date has been set for a week from Monday. Because of the violent nature of his attack on you while he was under a restraining order, they are not allowing bail until after that date. I was hoping I could get you to come home with me before he gets out."

"Do you mean you wanted me to just pack up and leave when I leave the hospital?"

"No, not really. I thought I could take you home tomorrow if you are released, then go back to Kentucky and prepare the kids for your homecoming, and then I could come back next weekend and get you. How does that sound?"

"That sounds wonderful. I need to be here a few days, give notice at work, talk to Greta and sort of take care of saying goodbye to my friends. Thank you for talking to the police. I was really scared of the idea of being at home alone with him out wandering around."

"You didn't need to worry about that. I had no intention of going back to Kentucky with the possibility of him coming back and hurting you." He took her hand. "I don't know what has happened to you or why we are at this point in our lives together, but I plan to be here for you from now on if you will let me."

"I will," she said meekly.

Finally it was time for visitors to leave, and Seth headed back to her house for the night. Katie felt safer and more relaxed than she had in a long time. She lay there thinking back over the last year in her life and it felt as if she had been in a sort of "twilight zone" for a long time. She had not been Katie. The fact that she'd taken on the name of Agatha was significant, for she had not really been Katie. She didn't know exactly who Agatha was, but it was someone alien to her. She had played a role for a while to avoid being Katie. Why hadn't she wanted to be Katie? Seth had made her want to be Katie again. She drifted off to sleep thinking of various things she and Seth had done over the years. She slept soundly until morning.

"Good morning, sleepy head!" said the bright-eyed nurse, entering her room with a tray of food. "Breakfast time."

"Wow, I must have been drugged. I slept like a log!"

"Well, you probably needed the rest," said the nurse. "And from what I hear, you may be going to be dismissed today. So you'll need your strength."

"I hope I get released. I'm ready to go home. I'm tired of this place," Katie said.

"What's this about being released?" the doctor said, entering the doorway. I never heard anything about being released."

"Well, everyone else thinks I'm going home," said Katie, smiling, "and I hope it's true."

"Actually, if everything looks good this morning, I'm thinking we may let you go home—that is, if you have someone to help you a bit for a day or so," the doctor said.

"Okay then, I guess that's a 'yes,'" said Katie.

By noon, all her lab results were back, the papers were all signed, and Seth was there to take Katie home. It felt good to have him there to help get her ready and drive the car up and help her into the car.

They drove home without saying much. Katie was reliving the night Kirk burst into her house as they pulled into the driveway. Suddenly she felt ill and when Seth stopped the car and came around to help her out, she froze. She burst into tears and told Seth she was afraid. He took her in his arms and finally she began to relax enough to get out of the car. He held onto her gently as they approached the steps, reassuring her that he would be right beside her. Still when she saw the livingroom she could not help but feel frightened. He walked her on through the living room and into her bedroom, where he helped her get settled on her bed.

"I think you've had enough activity for a while," Seth said. "Why don't you take a nap and I'll watch a little television?

When you wake up, we'll talk about getting something to eat for dinner."

Katie felt very tired all of a sudden as she pulled up the covers and relaxed.

When she awoke, it was nearly five o'clock. She couldn't believe it was so late, but when she heard the television, she eased out of bed and went into the living room.

"Be careful there, young lady, don't you fall," cried Seth. "Sometimes having a broken limb can cause you to get off balance."

"Of course," said Katie. "I'm okay. My leg's not broken, just my arm."

"I know. But still—" Seth began, then stopped. "I guess you're right. I just don't want you to be hurt."

Seth took care of her all weekend and was reluctant to leave her on Monday. "Are you sure Greta is coming this afternoon?" he asked. Katie was overwhelmed by his obvious concern for her. She remembered his tenderness the night before as they lay in bed together and his careful efforts not to hurt any of her bruised places.

"Yes, she promised to be here just after three and she's planning to spend the night," said Katie. "And besides I can do everything for myself if I need to. You've kind of spoiled me, but really I can get what I need."

"Well, I know, but--I'll just feel better knowing that someone is with you."

"I know what you're worried about. You're worried that Kirk might come back. But he's in jail. You said so yourself. He won't get out until after his court date."

"Okay, I guess you're right. I'd just hoped that there would not be any time for you to be alone today."

"Oh, just go on. I'll be fine," Katie said, confidently.

Seth came over to the couch where Katie was sitting and bent down to give her good-bye hug. He held her tight for a moment and kissed her soundly. "Take care, baby, and I'll see you on Saturday," he said.

"Bye," she called after him as he turned and walked toward the door.

As soon as Seth left, Katie went to the door and locked and bolted it. Then she went to the phone and dialed the police station.

"Nashville Police Department, this is Sgt. Reed," said a cheerful woman's voice.

"Could I speak to Inspector Kohn, please," asked Katie.

"He's not here right now," said the woman. "Could I help you?"

"Well, I just wanted to ... I mean I had a question about someone you have in custody, and I had talked to Inspector Kohn before," said Katie.

"Who is the inmate you're asking about?" asked Sgt. Reed.

"His name is Kirk Stone," said Katie.

"Let me check here," said the woman. There was a pause, and then she said, "Oh, he was released today. Have you tried his home?" Katie gaped. She could not say a word. She just sat there holding the phone. "Ma'am? Are you still there?" Sgt. Reed finally asked.

"Yes," Katie replied weakly.

"Is there anything else I can do for you?" the sergeant asked.

"No, thank you," said Katie and hung up.

CHAPTER 13

Katie gently laid the phone down and sat there, gathering her strength. Finally she stood up carefully and went to each of the windows and pulled down the shades in every room. She checked and rechecked the door locks both in the living room and the kitchen. Then she went into the bath room between the living room and kitchen (the only room in the house which seemed safe to her because the window was small and high), put the lid down on the commode, and, pulling her robe around her, sat down and cried. She must have sat there for hours, uncomfortable as it was. She felt frozen in a state of shock, fear, and unbelief. She knew no one to call or tell. She knew that her neighbor was out for the day. She knew that Greta was still at work, and Seth was driving home to Kentucky.

When the doorbell rang a few minutes before three, she jumped up so fast that she almost fell. Her feet and legs were numb and her whole body felt cold. She looked at her watch and realized that it was probably Greta, but she couldn't will herself to go to the door. She did, however, edge herself to the bathroom door and listen. After two rings, she heard Greta's voice. With relief, she went to the door and opened it.

Greta took one look at her and asked, "What in the world is wrong with you? You look exhausted…and a lot of other things."

Katie grabbed Greta, practically dragged her into the room and proceeded to lock all the locks behind her. She then looked up and said, "Kirk's out of jail." She began sobbing as Greta helped her over to the couch and made her sit down. Katie told her about how Seth had planned to return for her that weekend, thinking Kirk would remain in jail until then.

"Okay, gal, you're coming home with me," said Greta.

"I can't do that, Greta. I've got to pack all my stuff this week, and with my leg and arm so sore, I'm not even sure I could climb those stairs to your apartment."

"Well, you may be right. I guess I'll just have to stay with you then."

Katie looked hopeful. "Would you really do that?"

"Of course I'll do it! I will not leave you alone for one minute under any circumstances."

Katie stood, a little shaky, but feeling better. "Well, if you're sure, let's have a snack. I've got some fruit and cheese in the refrigerator, and there's soft drinks too."

While eating the snacks they began talking and continued until late evening. After a light dinner, Greta, said, "Why don't I start helping you pack?"

"Are you sure you want to start now? It's getting really late."

"I know. But I don't feel like either of us can sleep, so we may as well be productive!"

"Oh, I just realized I haven't had a chance to get boxes. How about cleaning out closets and stacking things in groups so we'll be ready to throw them in boxes when I get them?" Katie was excited about getting some things done now.

They were just finishing emptying the bedroom closet, when the phone rang.

Katie looked at her watch. "Greta, I can't answer that. What if it's Kirk?"

"I'll get it," said her friend, walking to the phone. "Hello."

Katie watched as Greta listened for a moment.

"Oh, Seth, it's Greta. I'll get her," she said and handed the phone to Katie.

"Hi, Seth. Did you have a good trip back?" Katie asked, trying to act as if everything was all right, wondering if she should tell him what she had learned. Obviously she did not succeed.

"Katie," Seth said, "What is wrong? Are you all right?"

"Well, yes and no," she confessed, realizing that she could not keep this from him. "After you left I called the police station, just to be sure that Kirk was still in jail, and they told me he had been released on bail."

"Oh, Katie, I'm so sorry. I should have done that myself," Seth said, worry in his voice. "I can come back tomorrow."

"No. No, I'll be fine. Greta has promised that she'll see to it that I have someone here until you come back this weekend. I've got a lot of packing to do, and Greta's going to help me. Anyway, he may not even show up. I certainly don't think he'd try anything if someone's here."

"Let me think about it. I'm just so shocked. They assured me that he would not make bail. I just can't believe this. This is crazy."

"I know. I didn't want to tell you, but after you obviously could tell that something was wrong, I decided you needed to know," said Katie.

"Of course I need to know. Tell you what—I'll be back by Friday, maybe Thursday afternoon. Tell Greta that if there is any problem having someone with you for her to call me and I'll just come on back. And Katie, you be careful, even with her there. Do not open your door for anyone unless you know for sure who it is. Okay?"

"Okay. I'll be fine. Thanks, Seth. I love you," said Katie.

"Love you too. Bye for now. I'll call you tomorrow," said Seth.

The next few days were busy ones, with Greta staying with Katie in the evenings, bringing armloads of boxes and packing supplies each day. Katie's neighbor came over each morning before Greta left and helped Katie pack during the day.

Just as Katie was getting dressed Wednesday morning, the phone rang and it was the police. "Mrs. Johnson, would it be convenient for us to come by later this morning and get a little more information from you? I know it's an intrusion, but the more we know, the better job we can do in court Monday."

"It'll be fine," said Katie. "I'll be here packing all day anyway."

"Okay, it's probably going to be late morning, maybe around 11:30. Is that all right?"

"That's fine," said Katie.

When the two officers arrived, one of them had obviously made a list of questions ahead of time, so he went down them quickly. As he put his note pad back in his pocket and stood to leave, he turned to Katie. "I know your plans are to leave this weekend, Mrs. Johnson, but I was wondering if you would consider staying over until Monday. As you know the court date is Monday morning, and I think our case would be strengthened if you were there."

"But why? You have all those pictures of what I looked like when I came to the hospital. Isn't that enough?"

"Technically, yes. But we just think your presence in the courtroom would add to the case. What do you think?"

"I definitely want Kirk held accountable for what he did. I don't won't anyone else to go through what I did, so I'll try to do whatever it takes to make that happen. I'll talk to my husband and see if he can stay over until Monday."

As soon as the officers left, Katie called Seth and told him what the officer had said. "Is that possible, for us to stay over?" she asked.

"I think so," Seth said. "I'm wondering about being away from Abby and Samuel that long though. It might work better for me to come on Friday instead of Thursday, though, if I'm going to be gone Monday too. Do you think Greta could stay until I get there on Friday? I definitely don't want you left alone."

"Yes, I'm sure she can. And even if something happened that she couldn't, my neighbor could probably come."

By Friday evening when Seth arrived, most of Katie's things were in boxes and she was feeling much improved. Her bruises were still obvious, but she looked much healthier than she had the week before, and it was obvious that she felt better. Knowing how worried Seth had been about her all week after learning about Kirk's release, she could tell that he was somewhat relieved when he saw that she was fine and was feeling so much better.

"Have you seen or heard *anything* from Kirk?" was the first question he asked.

"Not a word," said Katie.

"He wouldn't dare show up with big, bad Greta here," Greta said, laughing.

"Well, I would hope not," said Seth. "But you never know."

"Looks like you'll get a look at him on Monday," Greta said to Seth.

"They better keep an eye on me," said Seth, "or I might just take him on. I would like to punch his eyes out, let him try to fight someone other than a woman."

"Don't even think about it," said Katie. "I just want to get out of Nashville."

"I know," said Seth. "I'd probably not be able to hold my own in a fight anyway, but I tell you, I certainly feel like I'd like to try."

With most of the packing done on Saturday morning, Katie wanted to take Seth to visit and say goodbye to some of her friends that afternoon and then eat dinner at the restaurant where Katie had worked. Katie had already made plans to do some other sightseeing on Sunday, so she wanted to say her goodbyes on Saturday.

The first stop was a girl she had known since her first day at work. Jennifer Ford had been very helpful when Katie (Agatha) first came. Katie had not seen Jennifer much lately, but she still appreciated all her help. Greta had told all the girls at work about Katie's identity and her injuries.

"Come on in," said Jennifer, registering shock when she saw the still obvious bruises on Katie's face. "Coffee's almost made. This is my husband Donald." "Hi Jennifer and Donald. This is my husband Seth," said Katie, realizing for the first time how awkward this situation was. After a few moments, however, Jennifer, Donald, Seth, and Katie were talking like old friends, and Katie was proud of Seth's ability to adapt.

"I went to school with a guy from your area of Kentucky," said Jennifer. "He was from Somerset. I actually went to his home once."

"Yes, that's only about thirty miles from where I live," said Seth.

"Jennifer, you never told me that," said Katie.

"You never told me you were from Kentucky," said Jennifer, laughing.

"Oh, well, yes, I guess you're right," said Katie, blushing.

Everywhere they went that day they had similar experiences, with Seth surprising Katie with his casual acceptance of these strangers, and his acceptance of her having made new friends. Both of them sensed that this was a new beginning in their relationship, their ability to appreciate one another. When they finally arrived at the restaurant to eat, they were relaxed and hungry.

As soon as they entered, the hostess, a girl Katie had known for several months, ran over to greet them. She asked Katie (calling her Agatha) where she would like to sit. Seeing a corner booth empty, Katie asked for it. When they were seated Katie was pleased to see that Sophie, a good friend and a good waitress, was on duty.

"I hear the prime rib is scrumptious, so I'll take that," Seth said when Katie had ordered. Several employees came over to welcome her and Seth and tell her how sorry they were about all her troubles with Kirk. The atmosphere was good tonight, and Katie was a bit nostalgic to think she would not be returning to work.

"This place has great food," said Seth as he bit into a tender yeast roll.

"Of course," said Katie, "and great service," she added, winking at her friend.

"So I guess the servers expect great tips, too," said Seth. He laughed.

"Of course," said Sophie.

After they paid their bill and started back home that evening, Seth seemed to sense that Katie had mixed feelings. "Are you sad to be leaving your friends at work?" he asked.

"Oh, no, I'm fine. I'm glad to be going home," she said, afraid of hurting his feelings.

"It's okay to feel a little sad, you know," Seth said. "In fact, it would be unnatural not to have mixed feelings about leaving. I understand that these people have been there for you during a difficult time in your life. You don't need to be afraid to admit it."

"Thank you, Seth, for allowing me those feelings. Of course I have mixed feelings, but I'm not doubting what I want to do at all. I definitely want to go back to you and the kids."

On Sunday Seth and Katie slept late, had a big breakfast, and headed out to tour Nashville. At first they drove around several places where some of the country music stars lived, and down on music row where lots of the recording studios were located. She showed him the Ryman Auditorium and various other points of interest. They went to one of the malls for lunch and then went over to the Parthenon and walked around. They stayed out most of the day before heading back to her house. That night they finished packing the U-Haul they were pulling behind Seth's car, which was packed to the brim, leaving only the necessities for the night. As they were putting in some of the last things, Mrs. Anderson came over.

"Looks like you're just about ready to leave," she said. "I'm really going to miss having you there. It's the first time I've had a real neighbor, one I could relate to."

"I'll miss you too," said Katie.

"I was just wondering if you two would like to ride downtown with me in the morning," she offered. "That U-Haul's going to be difficult to navigate down around the courthouse."

"Oh we wouldn't want to inconvenience you," said Seth. "We'll manage."

"It won't inconvenience me," she said. "I have to go, too. I've been asked to testify."

"Oh, of course," said Katie. "I didn't think about that. Seth?"

"Okay, that's fine as long as you're going our way. I guess we'll all be basically on the same schedule."

"Yes, and I don't think we'll be there all that long. Since the hearing is at 9:00 and traffic is pretty busy at that time, we should probably leave about 8:00. Is that okay with you?"

"Sure, whatever you think," Seth and Katie said together.

The next morning when Katie got in Mrs. Anderson's car she was so nervous inside she was visibly shaking. She felt nauseous at the thought of seeing Kirk. Seth, sensing her anxiety, took hold of her hand and smiled at her. "You're going to be fine, Katie," he said gently. "It's Kirk that did wrong, not you. Just remember that. You are the victim, not the one at fault."

"I know, but I'm so scared," she said. "I just can't stand the thought of looking at him."

"We'll just stare him down," said her neighbor confidently. "Just stand up to him. Look him in the face and let him know who's in charge. He's a coward. He had no right to do you that way. We'll show him."

Their encouragement gave her a little confidence, but she still dreaded the moment when she actually saw him. She didn't know how she'd react. All she could think of was how mad he was the last time she saw him as he raged about in her living room. She hoped she wouldn't just collapse at the sight of him.

As they entered the courthouse, Seth held her arm tightly. Just before they entered Courtroom B, where they were having the hearing, Seth said, "Just remember we are right here with you. You are not alone."

His words were reassuring, and when she turned and saw Kirk, she felt nothing. Nothing. He stood there glaring at her, but all she felt was Seth's arm around her shoulders and her neighbor's reassuring hand on her elbow. When she sat down and looked at the other people there, their sympathy for her was palpable. No one in the courtroom (aside from Kirk and his attorney) blamed her for anything. The hearing went well. She did not have to say anything. Her neighbor verified that Kirk's car was there on the evening of the attack. Her attorney presented the restraining order that she had taken out prior to the attack. The policeman had given his deposition about his interview with her in the hospital and the other investigation he had done. Apparently Kirk did not try to deny that he had done it, seeming to think his actions were justified. When it was all over, Katie felt relieved that she would not have to see Kirk again. According to the police, he probably would not even ever know who she really was, because the information was never given to him about her name change, and she could go on back to her home in Kentucky a safe woman.

It was nearly noon when they finally got back to their car and pulled out of the driveway. Katie looked back at her neighbor waving from her front porch as they left. She felt that she was starting a life she had never known before, one which held many questions, but one in which her relationship with Seth would be richer and fuller than it had been before.

Driving along I-40 to Knoxville, Katie realized that she really didn't remember her drive to Nashville two years ago. The few days before and during her leaving were a blur. She tried to remember what it was like driving over this road, fleeing from her home and family, and she could not. The question of her future lay in her past. She and Seth had had a few good days in Nashville, and she knew he cared deeply for her, but something had snapped in her that day so many months ago, and she would not rest until she understood what it was. Several minutes passed with no conversation between them, each in their own world of thought.

As they neared Knoxville, Seth looked over at her and said, "Katie, today is the first day of the rest of your life," repeating a saying familiar to both of them.

"What will my life be like when I get home?" she asked.

"I'm not sure, but we'll make it work," he said.

"Tell me about your folks. What do they think? What have they said about me?"

"You probably don't want to know," he said, with the hint of a smile. "But I must say they have come around a little. I have assured them that we can work things out. I think in time, they'll be all right, but it may be difficult at first."

"What about the neighbors? Have you talked to any of them?"

Seth was quiet for just a moment too long. He seemed more uncomfortable with that question. "Well, I haven't talked to many, but I think it may be about the same with them as it is with my parents."

Katie was disappointed. "What about Brenda? Has she turned against me too?"

Seth seemed even more uncomfortable at that question. Quickly, he stammered, "No…no, I don't think Brenda has turned against you exactly. It's--it's just--well, you've been gone, and what could she do? She's just—I guess she doesn't know what to expect."

Finally, Katie got to an even more important question, which she had put off for as long as she could. "What about the kids? Tell me exactly what to expect. I need to know the truth."

"I know this will hurt, Katie, but you're right—you need to know the truth. Abby's really looking forward to your coming home, but she's a little afraid of what it will be like. She seems to hold the view that maybe you really don't care about her, and that's her big issue. She keeps asking, "Does Mama really want to see us? Does she still love me?""

"Oh, that's awful. I guess I understand that, though. I can show her how much I love her. I know I can. I'll just have to prove it by my every word and action. And Samuel, what about him?"

"Samuel is the big problem. He is very angry at you. In fact he has been putting up a big fight to go live with Mom and Dad."

"Oh, no! You're not letting him do that, are you? I mean I don't think I could stand that. I know I don't deserve to even be a part of the decision, but that would be terrible. How could I ever prove to him that I care about him if he didn't even live at home?"

"No, I have put my foot down about that. I told him that where he lives is not his decision at this point. The problem is that I think my parents have kind of encouraged that idea with him, telling him that he could live with them if he wanted to. But I told them that I would not permit it. Of course that just made him even madder, knowing that he had that option as far as they are concerned. But I've talked with my parents and encouraged them to support me in my decision, and I think they will. Anyway, it's going to be very difficult for you, and for him, at first. Don't expect miracles."

Katie gazed at the dash of the car as they drove. The full weight of all the problems facing her were now upon her shoulders. Perhaps she had traded one set of problems for an even greater one. She hardly noticed the scenery as they drove the last fifty miles toward home. The silence was not especially peaceful, but she needed it to gain strength enough to face her future. When they were finally on Highway 80 West out of London, she began to look around her and see familiar sights— well-known houses of friends, small stores, old barns. As they passed by the brick building housing the Royal Oaks elementary school where she had taught, she could visualize her room. Who was teaching the kids she might have taught had she stayed there? Had it only been two years? It seemed longer.

Soon they were turning into the driveway that was so familiar and yet alien. The red brick, two-story house looked spacious compared to the small house she had rented in

Nashville, and the lawn looked well-kept, as did those around it. No one came to the door. She saw a curtain move upstairs and a small head appear in Abby's bedroom window and then quickly disappear. Katie felt excitement, apprehension, and fear at the thought of seeing her children for the first time in nearly two years. Seth touched her arm, gave her an encouraging smile, and said, "Let's go in. We'll unload later."

As Katie approached the steps, the door swung open and a blond-haired Abby ran out the door and wrapped her arms around Katie, almost causing her to fall. "Easy, sweetheart," said Seth. "Don't knock her down."

"It's all right," said Katie awkwardly. "I'm so glad to see you. You've grown a foot since I saw you."

Abby backed off a little, and grinned shyly. "I know," she said. "Dad says I've grown…how many inches, Dad?"

"Two, I think," said Seth.

"Well, you've certainly grown some. I can tell," said Katie.

They all walked into the living room, and Katie noticed it was clean and orderly. "Why don't I get us something to drink and then we'll start unpacking the car. Abby, you can help with that," said Seth.

"Oh, can I? Great! I want to see all the stuff you brought home."

"Well, I'm not sure it's very interesting, but I do want you to help," Katie said while Seth was gone to fix the drinks. Katie heard voices in the kitchen, but could not understand what was said.

Then she heard Seth say, "I will not have you act like that."

In a moment, Seth pushed open the kitchen door with two glasses of lemonade in his hands. He offered Katie one and took a drink of his. As Katie looked at the room, she noticed that the furniture had been rearranged a little and that some of the pictures (including one of her by herself at the beach) had been removed from the table near the sofa. She looked up as she heard and saw the door to the kitchen open again.

"Mom, what happened to your face?" said a stern-faced Samuel as soon as he entered. Katie looked at Seth, not knowing how much he had told the kids. Seth said nothing, apparently wanting her to tell them as much as she felt like it. *Why had she not asked him about what they knew?*

"I ...a man attacked me and ...but I'm fine now, really," she stammered.

"Dad, why didn't you tell us?" said Samuel and Abby at the same time.

"Well, I didn't want to frighten you, and she is okay," said Seth. "Look, your mother really doesn't want to talk about that right now. She can explain it all at a later time. Right now we need to unpack the car, and the U-Haul trailer. I could use some help, Samuel."

"You said I could help too," said Abby.

"Of course," said her dad.

"Well, I'm supposed to go to Luke's to play basketball, you know," said Samuel.

"I know, but you've got time to help with this," Seth said, giving Samuel a stern look.

"Okay, okay," Samuel said sullenly and walked out the door toward the car.

The trip had tired Katie more than she thought, but she didn't dare not help. She began one of her many efforts to win back the respect of Samuel and Abby by doing over and above what she really felt like doing in order to show them that she was responsible and committed to her family.

With all four of them carrying boxes, bags, and packages, they had the car and the U-Haul empty in no time. When they carried in the last load it was getting late and Samuel quickly left the house to go to his friend's house, telling his dad that he would have dinner there and be there until bedtime, obviously wanting to avoid any more conversation with his mother.

"Mom left some lasagna and a salad in the refrigerator for dinner," said Seth. She had been there until just before Seth and Katie arrived. Katie wondered if Seth's mother left because she didn't want to speak to her, or if she did it because she knew Katie needed time alone with her family. Although Katie did indeed need to be alone with just Seth and the kids, she felt disappointed that Mrs. Johnson had not stayed to say hello to her.

That evening at dinner and for a while before bedtime Abby went back and forth between treating Katie like a visitor or a stranger and treating her like the mother that she had missed greatly and needed more than she could say. Katie wanted to take her in her arms and hold her, but when she got close, Abby seemed to back off and resist her efforts. Except for that moment when she first saw her and ran into her arms, Abby never really showed any affection for her. At bedtime, she made it clear that it was Seth and Seth alone she needed to help her get ready for bed.

Katie read the latest issue of *Reader's Digest* while Seth put Abby to bed. She read in a distracted state of mind, not really concentrating on what she was reading. As soon as Seth returned from putting Abby to bed, he called Samuel's friend's mother and told her to send Samuel home. A few minutes later, Samuel came through the front door, obviously unhappy that he had to be there. He closed the door soundly, just short of slamming it.

"We weren't through watching television," he said sullenly.

"You're never through watching television," Seth said. "Finish in your room."

"Samuel," said Katie, hesitatingly. "I…it's good to be home with you again."

"Yeah, well, I've got to go to bed," he said not looking at her.

As soon as he was out of earshot, Katie burst into tears. Seth sat beside her with his arm around her for a few minutes. "It's only the first day," he said. "He'll come around."

"I hope so. It's not that I would expect anything different. If it were me, I'd be the same way, angry. I have hurt all of you so much. The miracle is that you allowed me to come back at all," she said sniffling.

The kids had been off from school the Monday she came home because it was a teacher workday, but they had to go back to school the next day. Seth suggested that Katie stay in bed and just let him get them off to school as he usually did, but Katie wanted to be up and at least see what their routine had become. She was amazed at how competent he had become in assuring that the kids had breakfast and what they needed for school.

"Can I do anything to help you?" she asked several times, both to Seth and the kids. Each time the answer was "no." She felt like a stranger in her own home, which she was actually. When the children were gone, Seth began to get ready to go to work, and she realized that, since she sold her car before leaving Nashville, she had no way to go anywhere. They had decided that it would make more sense to sell it and use the money toward a newer model at home, instead of driving it home, since she was probably going to have to buy a newer one anyway once they got home.

"Seth, when can we get me a car?" Katie asked before he left.

"I was hoping to take a long lunch one day this week so we could look," he said. "Do you need one today? If so, you could take me to work I guess."

"No, I'll be fine. I just realized that I'd be home all alone all day with no way to get anywhere," she said. "I would love it if you came home for lunch though."

"Okay, I can do that," he said. "Oh, no I can't today. I promised my boss I'd have lunch with him and talk about hiring a few new guys. I'll call you right before lunch though and if you should need anything, here's my new phone number at work," he said, handing her a card with his number on it. "They changed it last fall."

The next few days were pretty much the same. Seth did all the parenting. Katie did little except clean up the dishes and make up their beds. At the end of the week, things were just as they were when she arrived. Seth had not found time to help her find a car, she had made no progress in dealing with the kids' attitude toward her, and although they had both been committed to finding a counselor who would continue her therapy as well as do some counseling with the whole family, it had not been mentioned. When Friday night came around, Abby said, "It's Friday night and we always go to the game on Friday night."

"What game?" she asked.

"The High School football game," she said, looking at her as if Katie were crazy.

"They didn't even have a football team when I went there," said Katie.

"Well, they do now," said Abby.

"You don't have to go if you don't want to," said Seth quickly. "I've just been taking the kids this fall. Since Samuel will be in high school next year, he likes to go and see some of his older friends who are playing."

Katie found herself wondering what everyone would think if she went, or if she did not go. One way or another, people would talk about her. She was sure that it would actually be easier on Seth and the kids if she did not go, but on the other hand, word may have gotten around that she was back, so people might wonder what she was doing and why she didn't come. It made her realize what an awkward situation she had created both for herself and her family.

"Katie?" said Seth. "Are you alright? It's really your decision completely. What do you want to do?"

"I guess I may as well go," she said, obviously not sure she was making the right decision. She was even less sure when she saw how sullen Samuel was all the way there. As soon as they got out of the car, Samuel took off, obviously hoping no one saw them get out of the car. Katie was sure he did not want his friends to see her with them. Well, she thought, he's just going to have to deal with the fact that I'm back. I can't be invisible.

She realized that even Seth was feeling a little awkward as they entered. He spoke hurriedly to some of the other adults, probably some of Samuel's friends' parents. They must be new, though, because she did not know them. When Seth finally said, "Oh, this is my wife, Katie," she could see the shock on their faces. She could not tell if it was because they did not know he had a wife, did not know she was home, or because her face still showed many bruises. She just spoke to them and walked on.

She did not particularly enjoy the game, not having grown up watching football, but she did notice that Abby seemed to really like having her there. She stayed right by Katie's side most of the time, and the only time she saw one of her classmates, she made a big show of making sure they knew Katie was her mother. It was really touching the way she seemed so proud of having her mother there. Katie really began to believe that Abby was warming up to her and hoped to see a big difference at home from then on.

"Welcome home," said a familiar voice from behind her while she was waiting in line at the concession stand during half-time activities. She turned around to face one of the high school teachers who had taught with her in the eighth grade about three years ago.

"Oh, thank you," Katie said softly, "It's good to be home."

"Well, I heard that you might be coming home, but I had no idea you were already back," the girl said. "It must be weird after all this time, just to come back home. How is it going?"

Katie sensed that the woman was hoping to get some good juicy gossip to spread to all her friends, so she kept her words to a minimum. "It is difficult, but things are going well," she said evenly. "Well I must get back to my place. It's good to see you."

The woman looked puzzled as Katie headed back to her seat without getting to the concession stand. Well, let her think what she wanted to, thought Katie, but she was not giving out any information for the gossip hens.

Katie made her way back into the stands, hoping she would not see any other familiar faces. She stayed close to Seth and

Abby the rest of the evening and just as they got settled into the car and she was wondering where Samuel was, he came out of nowhere it seemed and jumped into the car. They didn't talk much during the ride home. As soon as they got home, the kids went on upstairs to go to bed and Seth and Katie sat down and watched the news. When Seth turned the television off, Katie told Seth she needed to talk to him.

"Yes, what is it?" he asked.

"Well, we need to talk about some things. What am I supposed to do, now that I'm back? I just don't seem to be making any progress with the kids, I don't have a car to go anywhere, and I don't know what to do about getting a counselor as we discussed before I came back. I--we're—not really a family. I'm here, but I feel like I need a plan of some kind."

"What do you want me to do?"

"I don't really know. Maybe if we just get me a car, I can do *something.*"

"I guess we could go tomorrow and try to find one," said Seth. "As to the counselor business, Dad seems against that, especially for me and the kids. He says that's just nonsense. Why do we need a counselor? It was you who left. We are fine, me and the kids."

Katie looked at him. She couldn't believe he was saying this. He'd seemed so positive in Nashville. "Why are you against getting counseling? You were all for it last week in Nashville. This has got to have been very difficult for you and the kids, and they certainly aren't accepting me back as their mother. Don't you see how they'd need help with that?"

"Well, I don't know. I guess, but Dad says that people will think we're all crazy or something if we start doing that."

"But what do *you* say? That's what's important."

"I think we should give it a while. See if the kids come around. If things don't improve, or they get worse, then we can deal with it if we need to. I just hate for all the neighbors to be talking about us being nutty and everything, having to see a shrink."

"That's your dad talking, not you. It made perfect sense to you when we were in Nashville, and until you mentioned it to your dad. He's older and his generation of people didn't trust psychologists and psychiatrists, but people are more open to help like that now."

"I think you just want to talk this thing to death. All you need to do is just get a job, get back in the swing of things here at home, and everything will be fine. You'll see," said Seth confidently. "Anyway, let's plan to go tomorrow and look for a car."

"Okay then," said Katie. She was unhappy with this new attitude Seth had adopted since her return, but she didn't really know how to deal with it. She felt so much guilt for what she had done that she hated to argue with Seth, especially since he had been so willing to take her back. But even they had not had much intimacy. Sex, yes, but intimacy, no. She had thought they did when they were still in Nashville, but after they got home, he seemed to slip back into some of the old patterns they had established before she left. She just couldn't let that happen, yet she didn't know how to prevent it. When she got a car, she would begin on her own to make a plan for trying to find out why all this had happened in the first place. She didn't know exactly how, but she had to get a plan soon.

She went to bed that night exhausted, but looking forward to getting a car tomorrow.

CHAPTER 14

"What do you think, Abby? You think I should take this one?" asked Katie as they drove the latest in a string of different cars they had tried.

"I like it!" said Abby excitedly. The Chevrolet was only a year old and was a bright blue. The leather interior gave the car a sporty look and it was impeccable. Katie liked it better than any others they had seen, and she could tell that Seth liked it too. Samuel had refused to come along, opting to stay at home and watch television.

The car gave Katie a good feeling because it would allow her to come and go as she pleased, but also because she wanted to start asking some questions about her past. On Monday morning she set out to find some answers. She wanted to start with the little Royal Oaks School where she had attended as a child and where she had later taught. She knew a secretary and one teacher who had been there when she was a child. She thought that maybe they might remember something that would help her understand her past a little better. Maybe there was something that happened to her in school or during the time she went to the school.

Her first stop was the home of the secretary, Mrs. Allen. She was in her seventies and had been retired for a few years. She loved gardening, and all around her house were beautiful roses, tulips, and every kind of flower one could imagine. Katie had called that morning and asked to come by, so Mrs. Allen came out on the porch when she saw Katie drive up.

"Welcome, dear," said Mrs. Allen. "It's been a while since I've seen you."

"Mrs. Allen, I appreciate you seeing me. I don't know what you may have heard about me recently, but I'm sure you know that I left suddenly and no one knew where I was, not even my husband, for the last two years."

"Yes, I knew about all that. There's been lots of talk, but I don't pay much attention to that. I'm just glad you're back. Come on over here and sit down on the swing. You were always one of my favorites, even when you were a little girl in school," said Mrs. Allen.

"I appreciate that, Mrs. Allen. I know you've always been a good friend. That is really what I wanted to talk to you about, the time when I was in school. What do you remember about me when I was there?"

"You were the sweetest little girl. Your grandmother always dressed you neatly and you always did just what your teachers said. You were nearly perfect as far as I could see." Mrs. Allen rocked back and forth in the porch rocker padded with cushions. "Like I said you were always one of my favorites."

"Did I ever have any problems, or did you ever sense anything wrong at my home?"

"No, no, I always thought you were a very happy little girl. Of course your grandmother was a little older and she spoiled you a little, but not in a bad way. You just seemed to have everything you needed."

"And you don't remember any time when I might have been upset or had anything happen to me that caused people to be concerned?"

"No. None. Why do you ask that? Do you remember something?"

"I don't know. Maybe not," said Katie. "You know I've been seeing a counselor in Nashville, where I was living."

"Oh? I didn't know you'd been in Nashville. Did you see many country music stars while you were there?"

"Unfortunately, no. I worked most of the time, and I only saw Johnny Cash once when he and his son came into the restaurant where I worked. But anyway, back to my question. I was seeing a counselor, and he seemed to think that there might have been something in my past that had made a great impact on me, but I had forgotten about it. You know my grandmother that raised me is dead. So I just thought that maybe I could learn something about my past through you or some other person who knew me."

"What about your dad? Why don't you ask him? He should know."

"Oh, he's in a nursing home over in Corbin, but they say he hardly knows anything. They say he's in really bad shape. I know I need to go visit him, but I don't expect he'll even recognize me."

"Well, I'm afraid I'm not much help because I never saw or heard anything unusual about you while you were in school. Now Mrs. Hopper, she lives over on Owl Creek. She was your

133

first grade teacher. Maybe she remembers something that I didn't know about. She may be getting a little forgetful now, but she has a pretty good memory about stuff back then. She just can't always remember what she did yesterday. You know what I mean?"

"Yes, I do. That's the way Grandma was before she died. My aunt Esther is probably the only relative that could help me. I may have to talk to her at some point. I do plan to talk to Mrs. Hopper also. In fact, I'm planning to go there tomorrow. She said she was going to the doctor today. I really appreciate you talking to me," Katie said as she stood to leave. "I'll be going now, but if you don't mind, I may come and visit again. I've really enjoyed visiting with you."

"You come back any time, honey. I don't get too many visitors, and I'm not able to get out much. My knees hurt a lot, so I can't get around very well, but I enjoy company."

That night Katie told Seth about her visit to Mrs. Allen.

"So did you learn anything important?"

"No. Not really, but I did get an idea. I think I need to spend some time with Aunt Esther. She was around when I was little and spent a lot of time at Grandma's. She was Grandma's younger sister, and I think Grandma was almost like a mother to her. She lived across the road, but except for sleeping at her house, she was at our house most of the time. Her mother, Mammie, was getting pretty old, and she was kind of mean, I thought, to Aunt Esther. Maybe she was just old and cranky. But anyway, Esther just came over to our house about every day it seemed. I don't know why I had not thought about talking to her before. I guess she's the one person who would know if anything had happened to me, but I just never thought about it. Anyway, I thought I'd go over there Wednesday if it's okay with you."

"That's fine I guess. I was just wondering, are you planning to apply for a job now that you're back? It's been a little hard financially without a second income, you know," Seth said.

"Yes, I want to work eventually, but I have so many issues to work out. My main concern is to regain my kids' confidence, and that will be harder if I don't have any time to spend with them."

"Well, we can wait a few months, I guess if you need time," said Seth.

The next day Katie was looking forward to seeing Mrs. Hopper. She believed that surely if there had been anything in her childhood that was traumatic Mrs. Hopper would have known about it, or at least known that something had happened. That morning she was determined to help the kids with their breakfast and see them off to school.

"Seth, I'll fix breakfast for the kids. You just go on and get a shower," she announced.

"Are you sure? You know Abby likes her eggs just so-so, and Samuel never eats either eggs or toast. He likes cereal, and…"

"I know all that. I've been watching the last few days. I can do it," Katie insisted.

"Okay then, but don't be surprised if Samuel is super critical."

"I've just got to get back into the routine with them, Seth. No one can do it for me, and I'll just have to take whatever they dish out. Go, get on to your shower."

About ten minutes after Seth headed upstairs, Samuel and Abby came into the kitchen as Katie was finishing making the eggs and toast for Abby.

"Where's Dad?" Samuel asked as soon as he entered the room.

"He's getting a shower," said Katie. "Are you drinking milk?" She directed her question to Abby, but Samuel had his back to her.

"I hate milk," he said, as if he'd been insulted.

"I was talking to Abby. What do you want to drink?" she asked, trying to keep calm and not let him get to her.

"I'll get it," Samuel said sullenly, opening the refrigerator door and pulling out a carton of orange juice.

When she reached for the cereal, he grabbed it before she could get it and fixed his own cereal, which was fine with Katie, except that he did it as if it were an act of defiance. Although Abby did not complain or say anything unkind, she looked at her eggs and toast and barely touched them. She thought they looked just like they had the morning before when Seth had fixed them, and Abby had wolfed them down as if they were great. Katie walked to the door with her when she was ready for school and gave her lunch money and two library books. Abby just looked up the stairs as if willing her father to be there.

After Seth left that morning and she had straightened up the kitchen, Katie went upstairs and made beds and picked up clothes and towels. Later that morning she put a roast on for dinner that evening so that she would have the afternoon to visit with Mrs. Hopper. She was hoping that spending more time in homemaking activities would make the kids see that it was better that she was back, but in reality she knew it would take much more than that. She was convinced that the whole family needed counseling, but it was obvious that Seth had decided he was not going to pursue it. She would have to seek individual counseling, at least at first. Maybe later on, she could talk Seth into it.

When she arrived at Mrs. Hopper's that afternoon, she was surprised at how much the older woman had aged. But Mrs. Hopper made her feel welcome immediately as she opened the door.

"Well, look who's here! I had totally forgotten you were coming. Come on in and have a seat. I'm sorry I'm not dressed. I'm just here by myself so much that I just stay comfortable. Land sakes, child, you look pretty! You know I have a picture of you when you were a little girl—you and a bunch of other kids in front of the school. Let me see, what did I do with that? I was just looking at it yesterday, but I don't know where I put it." She started looking around the room for it, but could not find it. Finally she came back and sat down on the couch.

"Mrs. Hopper, you do know who I am, don't you?" asked Katie.

"Oh, yes, of course. You're Katie Royal."

"Mrs. Hopper, you taught me in the first grade, didn't you?"

"Yes, and in the third grade too, as a matter of fact. You were one of my favorites. You could read better than any kid in the third grade."

"Did you know my grandma?"

"Oh, yes, she came to the school quite often. She was crazy about you. I mean she made you mind, but I could always tell that she loved you very much. What ever happened to her?"

"She's been dead about ten years now. She just had a heart attack in her sleep I reckon. Anyway, one of the neighbors went over there one morning to help her with some chores, and found her dead."

"Oh, I didn't know that."

"Mrs. Hopper, when I was in school, did anything bad ever happen to me that you remember?"

"Bad? No, not that I remember. Why?"

"Well, I just wondered. You know, sometimes your mind plays tricks on you, and it seems like maybe there's something that happened to me when I was little that I just almost remember, but can't."

"And you thought it was bad?"

"Maybe. Or scary. I'm not sure."

"I don't remember anything that involved you. I remember one time your father came to school to pick you up for some reason, and the next day your grandmother came to see me. She seemed rather angry and told me that I was not to let you go with him if he ever did that again. He never did, but I wondered why that was. She gave no explanation and I didn't ask."

"Well, my dad drank a little, so maybe she thought he might not drive safely," Katie said.

"Maybe so. I always thought you had a good life, and you always seemed happy," Mrs. Hopper said musingly.

"I did have a good life as far as I can remember. Grandma was a good woman. She practically raised her sister, Aunt Esther, and then she raised me. Aunt Esther always seemed kind of sad, and she was there a lot. She married once for a while, and then later, when her husband left her, she came back home, and again she spent a lot of time with Grandma, even before her mother died. My great-grandma was sort of cranky and Grandma was always pleasant to be around. When she

138

died, Aunt Esther said it hurt her much more than it did when her mother died."

"I don't think I ever knew your Aunt Esther. I heard you talk about her though when you were little. You talked about her like she was an older sister who knew everything. You'd say, 'Esther said...'' and then you'd act as if no one should question it anymore," Mrs. Hopper said, laughing at the memory.

"I really looked up to her in those days. We kind of drifted apart when she married and was gone a while, and we never got as close again, because by the time she returned home, I was older and spending more time with friends and in school activities. But I still love her. I'm planning to go visit her later this week."

"You should. I'm sure she'd be happy to see you. How are things going for you at home now?"

"Well, I'm glad to be back, but it's difficult. Do you know of any good counselors, psychologists, around here?"

"I don't know any personally, but do you remember Mrs. Haynes that taught school here right after you started high school?" As Katie nodded that she did, Mrs. Hopper continued, "Her son-in-law is a psychologist or psychiatrist, and he has set up a practice over in Somerset, I think. I've heard that he's really good, and my cousin's daughter has been seeing him. I can't remember his name, but I could get it for you if you'd like."

"That would be great. I was seeing a therapist in Nashville, and he promised to give me the name of someone around here, but I never actually got the name. It would be even better to get a recommendation from someone who actually knows him. If you will find out his name, I'll call you later in the week. Oh,

Mrs. Hopper, would you mind not mentioning this to anyone? Some people are rather funny about psychologists and other mental health professionals," Katie said, getting up to leave.

"Oh, I know, Katie. That's the way it's been with my cousin and her family. They've kept it rather quiet. I won't mention it to anyone, dear," said Mrs. Hopper, following Katie to the door.

When Katie left she felt a little disappointed that she had not learned anything significant from Mrs. Hopper, but she reasoned that she should have known that would be the case. If something had happened to her after she was in school, she would probably have remembered it. Maybe something had happened when she was much younger. She really didn't remember much about her life before she went to school. She was convinced that the key to understanding her background lay in the little community in which she grew up. Not too many people still lived there that she knew, but there were some. And there was Aunt Esther of course. She surely would know something about Katie's early life. She was there all the time.

Katie approached the house planning to tell Seth that she wanted to spend time with Aunt Esther before she took a job. As she got out of the car, she saw that Seth was already home from work, which was rather unusual, and she was pleased that she would have more time to talk to him. Entering the living room, she saw Seth sitting on the couch with his head down.

"Seth, I have a great idea about how to…" she stopped in mid-sentence when she saw that Samuel was sitting across from his father glaring defiantly at them both.

CHAPTER 15

"Katie, we've got a little problem here," Seth said.

"What do you mean?" she asked.

"It's not any of her business," said Samuel to his father.

"She's your mother, son, which makes it very much her business," said Seth.

"You're making this a much bigger thing than it really is," said Samuel.

"Theft is not a big thing? Since when?" Seth said, standing up.

"Will you just tell me what's going on?" asked Katie.

"Samuel was caught with money—a good bit of it actually—that he obviously took from another student's book bag," Seth said.

"But why? Samuel, why would you do that?"

"It's none of your business. You don't have a right to criticize me."

"I'm not criticizing you. I'm just asking you a question. Why would you steal someone else's money?"

"Well, at least I didn't just leave, like you did!" he almost shouted, and ran up the stairs to his room.

Katie and Seth sat and said nothing for a few minutes, and finally Seth said, "Katie, maybe you should just let me handle this."

"Seth, Samuel is a very troubled and angry young man, and I'll agree that I am mostly to blame for the way he is, but we've got to get some help for him. I mean counseling. Okay, I'll let you handle it, but you can't go on ignoring his need for help. I'm getting the name of a counselor from Mrs. Hopper, and when I do, I really hope you'll support me in making an appointment for both me and Samuel—maybe all of us. I know your father and mother don't want that, but they do not have to live in this house." Seth gave a big sigh and walked into the kitchen, not responding to her request.

The next morning Seth took Samuel to school and although she never heard exactly what happened, apparently they returned the money and the matter was settled. It was never mentioned again, but the school must have told Seth that if Samuel's record were cleared he would have to agree to counseling.

"Katie, I guess we'll have to do what you said, get some counseling for Samuel. So whenever you get the name of that person, go ahead and make him an appointment. And be sure that the school principal knows that you are taking him." Katie was thrilled to hear this, although she wished that Seth had agreed to it on his own, without pressure from the school. As it turned out, though, it was probably a good thing since Samuel was reluctant to go but knew that he had to since it was a condition of clearing his discipline record.

"This is stupid. Why do I need to go talk to some stranger about things that he knows nothing about?" Samuel grumbled the morning of his first appointment.

"Sometimes strangers are the best people to talk to," said Katie. "They don't know anything about you except what you tell them, so you can be completely honest and you have someone who listens to your every word. When I was in Nashville, and realized what a terrible thing I had done to you, your sister, and your dad, I went to a counselor."

"Well, bully for you! It didn't help us any," said Samuel derisively.

"Maybe not, but it did help me, and it's the reason I was able to return home," Katie said, on the verge of tears.

"And I guess you think you did us a big favor by coming home? I don't recall asking you to come back," he sneered.

"Samuel!" Seth said, entering the room. "I will not tolerate any more of those kinds of remarks! You are free to think whatever you want, but you will not talk to your mother like that. Do you understand?"

"Yes, sir," Samuel answered.

Katie left the room quickly and went upstairs. She had a brief cry, and then finished getting ready. This was not the first time Samuel had made angry remarks to her, and she knew it would not be the last. She appreciated Seth's efforts to make him be civil to her, but at the same time she knew she deserved some of the anger. If only she could understand more of why she had acted the way she did, maybe Samuel could understand and someday be able to forgive her.

Her own appointment with Dr. Adams had been the day before Samuel's. She had wanted to meet the psychologist and get to know him before she took Samuel. She was very impressed with him and his manner. She had called and asked her counselor in Nashville to correspond with Dr. Adams a few days before, so when she went she did not have to tell him the whole story, and Dr. Adams was very helpful on her first visit. When she told him of her plan to visit in the community in which she grew up, he was supportive of her efforts, but told her not to expect miracles, and to give herself time. If her childhood did hold some secret that had caused her to run away, it might take months, even years to uncover the truth.

"Why can't Dad take me to see this guy?" Samuel asked as they got into the car to leave.

"He has to work. Anyway, I think he prefers that I take you. I'm not sure why that is, but I'm glad to take you," Katie said as pleasantly as she could. They drove mostly in silence, with Katie asking an occasional question about Samuel's schoolwork, and Samuel answering in monosyllables mostly. He had brought a book or two and a notebook, and he did a little homework as they rode.

When they got there, she went in the waiting room with him. When Dr. Adams came out and invited him in, Katie introduced them and then sat down and read a magazine. She prayed that Dr. Adams would be able to connect with Samuel in some way, but wasn't too optimistic. Maybe over time it would happen. The school had recommended that he see Dr. Adams twice a month for at least six months. They didn't actually say that he had to go for six months to clear his record, but they implied that was the case, and Samuel had accepted that as the agreement. Katie felt that if there should be some major breakthrough before then and Dr. Adams felt that he did not need to see him, the school would accept that.

"How did it go?" Katie asked when they got back in the car.

"He said that I didn't have to tell you anything," Samuel said, smugly, as if he felt that Dr. Adams was siding with him against her. Secretly that pleased her, but she did not allow herself to reveal that.

"Well of course, that's always the case with counselors," she said. "That's the reason it's safe to talk to them. What's said in their office stays there. Otherwise, people would not go to them long."

"Well, it's not going to do any good anyway. He can't possibly understand me. He just sits there and looks like he's bored most of the time, which I guess he is. I lead a boring life," said Samuel. "Can I change the radio station to something good?"

"Sure," said Katie. "Whatever you want to listen to." This seemed to please Samuel and for the first time that day he didn't look angry as he tuned in to the loud rock music.

The next time Katie visited Dr. Adams, she had just had a big fight with Samuel that morning and she was distraught. After listening to her tirade for about fifteen minutes, Dr. Adams looked at her and said, "Did you ever think that his anger might be a healthy thing? That maybe Samuel has a right to be angry and needs to express it to you in order to move on?"

"I know he has a right to be angry, but I guess I never thought of it as being a good thing. I just find it hard to accept," she said.

"Of course it's hard to accept. But you left him at an important time in his life and he had no idea that one morning he'd wake up and have no mother to do all those little things that mothers do for a child. You did not even say goodbye, so it would be unnatural for him to just be okay with that," said Dr. Adams.

"But how do we get past it? How do I prove myself again?" she asked.

"That's a question that is hard to answer, but I'll tell you that it may take a while, so don't expect it to happen overnight. Also, don't expect me to 'fix it,' to make him all right with you again. But if you persist, it may eventually happen."

"It 'may' eventually happen? You mean he may never forgive me?"

"I don't know. That's up to him. He's a person, Katie. You can't make a person forgive you," Dr. Adams said. "Even if it's your son, he has to make the decision. You can try as hard as you can, but in the end, it's his decision to make."

Katie felt as if she were going to cry. Dr. Adams let his words soak in for a while. Then he said, "But I do think you're doing the right thing. You're talking to him as much as he will allow, and not being judgmental. And you're working toward understanding yourself and your actions. That's about all you can do. Maybe continuing to focus on understanding yourself will eventually lead to reconciliation with your son, but you can't get too wrapped up in making amends with him, because you have little control over his thoughts about it. Tell me about your plans to go visit your...aunt, is it?"

"I'm hoping to go over there next Monday. I talked to my Aunt Esther on the phone. She can't hear too well, but she knows I'm coming. While I'm there I may visit some of the other folks that I knew as a child." Katie brightened a little as she related to Dr. Adams a little about her aunt and the relationship with her, telling him that she believed her aunt might be able to tell her what happened that was traumatic.

"Remember what I told you earlier, Katie. If something did happen during your early years that caused you to repress the whole experience, it is probably not something your aunt will just spill to you the first time you ask her. There was a reason it was never mentioned, and although your aunt might know something, she may find it very difficult to discuss with you. It's also possible that something could have happened to you that she never knew about, or she too could have repressed it. She was quite young at the time, you know, adults of that generation did not discuss things as openly as they do today. These things can get complicated, you know," he said.

Despite his words, Katie was looking forward to spending time with Aunt Esther. Esther had always been Katie's favorite, but she always seemed rather sad. She was always kind to Katie though, and she would take her on long walks and sometimes they'd take a picnic basket and go down by the creek and sit or hours, tossing pebbles in the creek, wading up to their knees, and watching the birds, frogs, and other living things. Esther would point out unique features of the frogs or birds to Katie and they would sit quietly until it got late in the afternoon and Esther would pack up their basket and they walk home in time for supper.

CHAPTER 16

Monday morning Katie got a call from Aunt Esther saying that she had come down with a stomach virus and she'd better postpone her visit a few days. Katie was disappointed, but told her aunt that she understood. When Seth heard the news, he seemed sympathetic with her disappointment. When he was ready for work, he hesitated a moment at the door.

"Katie, I know that you had planned to go see your Aunt Esther this week, but since that is not working out, maybe you could look for a job. I looked at all our bills last night and I'm just not making enough to sustain another car payment and keep up with everything on one salary. I'm sorry," he said, and she believed he really meant it.

"You know they won't let me teach again," she said.

"Yes, I know, but maybe if you talked to Carl Royal he could help. He's a distant cousin of yours, isn't he?" As she nodded, he continued, "You know they've made him principal at the school now. Maybe he might have something, even clerical or an aid to start."

149

"Oh. So he was the one who worked out the deal with Samuel's discipline problem. I didn't realize it was Carl." She sat there a moment. "I just hate to use the fact that I'm a relative to get the job. It's just so embarrassing."

"I know, but you've got to start somewhere, and at least he might be a little more sympathetic. If you did get a job there, maybe you could later convince them to let you teach. I don't think they actually ever took it to the state to revoke your license. There was mention of it, but fortunately the superintendent was against it. His position seemed to be that since they did not know why you left, they did not know whether your reason was legitimate. Anyway, if you could convince Carl to hire you for anything it would be a start."

"Okay, I'll try," she said, realizing with disappointment that it might be a while before she could go see Aunt Esther.

The rest of the week, though, she postponed going to the school. She couldn't stand the idea of walking back in the school and seeing people staring at her with chastising eyes. She also felt that the kids, especially Samuel would hate having her there. It would add to their embarrassment and humiliation. Therefore, she went everywhere but to the school. Everywhere she went, she felt piercing eyes and condescending attitudes. Even people she didn't know soon figured out who she was and shook their heads as if to say, "No, of course we wouldn't hire someone who just walked out on her last job as well as her family."

At the end of the second week, dog-tired, she finally gave in and told Seth she was going to call Carl the Monday morning. She had almost worked herself into an anxiety attack by the time she heard his voice.

"Hello, this is Carl Royal," he said in a very professional voice, unlike the voice of Coach Royal, the 'good ole boy.' "How can I help you?"

"Carl, this is Katie Johnson," she said.

There was a slight hesitation, just enough for Katie to realize that Carl was surprised. She had intentionally not identified herself to the receptionist, and fortunately the young lady had not asked for her name. "Katie," he said, "…uh, it's been a while since I've heard from you. When did you get back home?"

"A few weeks ago. Carl, I know you're busy, so I won't keep you, but I was wondering if I could come and talk to you sometime," she said breathlessly, revealing her uncertainty.

"Well, no harm in that, I guess. But Katie, I hope you understand that I could not hire you back as a teacher. Even if I wanted to the Board would never approve it," he said.

"Oh, I know that, Carl. I just wanted to talk to you." She didn't know if she should mention about him hiring her in some other capacity. She was afraid if she did he might not agree to talk to her at all.

"Let's see, I've got meetings all day today, and tomorrow I'm going to be out of the office. How about Wednesday morning, say around 10:00?"

"I'll be there," she said, disappointed that things were moving so slowly, but at least she could talk to him. Carl was a good guy, and she thought he would be helpful, but she had not really thought of the fact that it would not be totally up to him. The Board would have to approve it, and they just might not want her in any capacity. She had called her aunt after she had to start job hunting to tell her she would not be able to come visit for a while. She thought of calling her and planning to go out the next day, but decided against it. She wanted to wait until she had time to focus on what she wanted to learn when she went to visit. Now she was so involved in job hunting that she just couldn't believe it would be helpful to go at this time.

She called an acquaintance who owned a restaurant in London to see if they might need help. At first the manager, who had no idea who Katie was, said, "Oh we're always looking for good waitresses. Let me let you talk to the owner of the restaurant."

As Katie's hopes began to rise, the owner came on the phone and identified herself. When Katie said her name, there was a long pause, and then the owner said, "I'm sorry Katie, we have no openings right now, and our staff is pretty stable— don't have many employees leave once they sign on. Good luck." It was the same most everywhere she applied. The word seemed to have gotten out.

When Wednesday morning came, Katie felt that it might be her last hope for any kind of job, so she tried to look her best, even if for a distant cousin who would probably not notice. Seth, noting her apprehension, said, "Katie, don't get discouraged. Even if this doesn't work out, something will work out. There are many places you have not contacted yet."

"I don't know. Everywhere I've gone, as soon as people learn who I am, they just close me out. I don't know what we'll do if no one will give me a second chance."

Seth gave her hug, and said, "Hang in there, honey. It'll be all right."

Despite Seth's encouragement, Katie was still anxious as she walked down the hall toward the principal's door. When she entered the receptionist's area, it was obvious that the young girl either remembered her or had been told who she was. She was pleasant enough though, and rang Carl immediately announcing Katie's arrival.

"Katie, it's good to see you," Carl said enthusiastically as she entered. He seemed genuinely glad to see her, and that made her feel better immediately. Suddenly she remembered a church picnic when they were teens. He was two years older than she and they had all played volleyball in back of the church. Somehow her foot had gotten caught in a root sticking out of the ground and she had fallen. Most of the teens had burst out laughing at her lying on the ground, but Carl had run over and asked her if she was okay and then helped her up. Well, she needed picking up again, so maybe he would come to her rescue.

"Carl, I don't want to put you in an awkward position, but I really need a job, and things aren't looking too good for me now. I'm willing to do anything. I'm not asking for a teaching position," she finished, giving him a pleading look.

He sighed. "I've been thinking about this ever since you called, Katie, and I'd really like to help you. I've always liked you and Seth too. But if I'm going to ask the Board to approve you for any position at this school, I will need to feel that I understand a little more about what made you break a contract with the system at a terrible time—and leave your family too. They will have to be convinced that it won't happen again, and I can't convince them unless I am convinced. So I need you to talk to me a little about why this happened and why you feel that it won't happen again."

Carl was a much more mature and perceptive person than she had thought he was. She was impressed with his thinking and she could not fault him for what he was asking.

"To begin with, I'm not sure I can tell you exactly why I left, except that I was very depressed at the time, and some things happened that, while they probably wouldn't make sense to anyone else, they sort of caused me to run. Well, let's just say that I was very depressed and I could not deal with all my responsibilities at home and at school at the time." She stopped for a moment, and then looked up at Carl.

"Go on," he encouraged.

"Now let me explain why it will not happen again. First of all, while I was away, I had the good sense to recognize that what I did was senseless and basically unforgivable, so I went to a therapist to try to get myself back on track."

"And did you? Get yourself back on track, I mean?" Carl asked.

"Well, that part I'm still working on," she continued. "I have now found a counselor over in Somerset so I can continue to work on my own problems," she said.

"That will be a point in your favor, I think," he said. "Have you come to any understanding about what happened? Why you might have gotten depressed, or what could have caused you to get to the breaking point?"

"Well, yes and no. Carl, how well did you know my folks when we were growing up? Did you ever know of anything traumatic that happened to me or my family?"

"Why, no, not that I think of. I mean your family was kind of weird as far as I was concerned, but I never thought it bothered you in the least. You always seemed happy and your grandma was the sweetest person I've ever known. She always mothered anyone who got near her," he said laughing.

"How were we weird? What do you mean?"

"Well, I always thought it was strange that you lived with your grandma, when your dad and stepmother lived right next door practically. And your aunt, she practically lived at your grandma's too. So I thought all the other adults had it made with your grandma taking care of all the young ones. I don't know, I just thought that was strange, but it didn't seem to bother any of you."

"It does seem rather strange now, but at the time it didn't, not at all. I'll have to ask Aunt Esther what she thinks. Anyway, back to my efforts to learn the source of my problems. The reason I ask about what you knew was that right before I left I had some—flashbacks, I guess you'd call them, when I remembered something very upsetting or scary to me, but I'm not sure what it was. It was like I was having panic attack of some sort, but I couldn't figure out why. I know this makes no sense, but I'm convinced that I was remembering something that had frightened me or hurt me badly when I was little. Anyway, I plan to go to my aunt and maybe some other people where I grew up and see if I can find out if something happened to me that I can't remember, but it's hidden somewhere, you know, in my subconscious. I think if I could identify it, I could get passed it and could assure people, even my kids, that it wouldn't happen again. That's all I know to tell you."

"I think that the Board might be willing to give you a second chance with my recommendation. I would of course have to tell them that you have had counseling and are continuing the counseling here. You don't object to that do you?"

Katie brightened at his words. "No, certainly not. Do you have anything in mind?"

"Well, we have an aide in the primary grades whose husband has taken a job over in Western Kentucky, and they will be moving in three weeks. Would you be interested in doing that for a while?"

"As I said earlier, I'll do anything. The advantage to that would be that I would not be working close to either of the kids' classrooms. I was a little concerned about how they would feel about me being here, but since they would probably not even ever see me during the day, it would be better."

"I won't be able to get it before the Board until next week, and I don't know how they'll respond, but I'll try," Carl promised.

"I really appreciate this," said Katie. "I will always be grateful to you."

"I'm glad to do it for you. Tell Seth hello for me. And Katie, I'm sorry about the trouble with Samuel a few weeks ago. I guess this has been very difficult for him."

"Yes, and it still is. I'm hoping the counseling will help, but so far I can't see much improvement. Abby seems to be doing fairly well with my return, but Samuel continues to be angry and resentful. I don't blame him, but it's very difficult sometimes."

"Well, hang in there. Samuel's a good kid. He's just got to work through everything and he's at an age when a lot's going on in his life." As Carl showed her to the door, he put his arm around her shoulders in a show of support. "I'll call you as soon as I know anything."

Katie was excited when she told Seth about her interview with Carl. "I know that something could go wrong. The Board might not approve me, but Carl seemed optimistic that they would. Anyway, it sure made me feel better."

"How do you feel about working as an aid in the primary grades?" Seth asked.

"I guess at this point I just look at it as an opportunity to have a job with the system at all. Naturally, I like working with older kids better, but I knew they wouldn't hire me as a teacher, and it's probably better for the kids that I'm not working where I have contact with them, especially Samuel."

Wednesday morning about 8:30 Carl called with the good news that the Board had approved her at their meeting on Tuesday night. Katie was to come on in on Thursday morning to work with the other aid for a few days before she left.

Entering the front door the next morning, Katie noticed a few glances from other employees as she walked over to sign in with the assistant principal, a young man who looked like he was just out of college. "Good morning Mrs. Johnson," he said. "I'll take you down to the first grade hall. I know that you're familiar with the school, but Carl said he did not think you'd met Miss Patton." He was polite, but he did not say much going down the hall, and he acted as if he had no interest in getting to know her or helping her. He was just doing what he had been told to do.

"No, I don't believe so," said Katie, feeling more uncertain than she'd felt in a long time.

Miss Patton was another young 'just out of college' teacher, but Katie liked her instantly. She welcomed Katie graciously, and showed no signs that she knew or cared why Katie had taken the job. She did recognize the fact that Katie had taught school, but she appeared to think that was a major bonus for her. She introduced Katie to Susan, the aide who was leaving, and was able to make them both appear to be the most wonderful assets that she could have. Susan, too, was welcoming and showed Katie around the room where all the supplies were, and introduced her to each of the children as she worked her way around the room. By the end of the morning Katie felt like she'd been there at least a week.

As they escorted the children to the cafeteria, she heard a soft voice say to someone, "There she is. Did you hear…." Katie longed to be back in the classroom where she had felt safe and appreciated.

Despite the little incident in the hallway, over all Katie felt good about her first day at work, and especially about the young teacher with whom she would be working. After school that day, she stayed with the teacher to see all the children on their buses and talked to her about her expectations in regard to several of her duties.

When Katie started to leave that day, she gathered her things together and then said, "Miss Patton, do you know my background and why I'm not teaching?"

"Yes, Mr. Royal told me about you before you came, Mrs. Johnson. You don't need to worry about me. I'm just glad to have someone with the experience you've had in teaching to help me. I love Susan, but I'm looking forward to having someone who knows a little about education in here with me." She paused. "I guess all of us have thought of doing what you did at one time or another," she said, smiling softly. "Maybe we just didn't have the courage." Giving Katie a little hug, she went down the hall toward the office as Katie left.

Katie approached the sign that said "Royal Oaks School" with a little more confidence the next morning and proceeded down the hall to Miss Patton's classroom where she got right to work.

"Miss Katie, Miss Katie, do you have any children?" the bright-eyed little blonde girl said, tugging on Katie's sleeve.

Smiling down at the little girl, Katie said, "Yes, as a matter of fact I do. I have two, a boy and a girl, both older than you are."

"I thought so," said the little girl. "You know just how to treat little kids. You remind me of my mother."

Katie helped the little girl with her work and moved on to another table. She found that helping these children made her gain some confidence that she could relate to her own kids. After her long experience of being depressed and then leaving her family, she had lost confidence in herself as a mother. Being able to relate to these children gave her hope.

After a week of working at the school, Katie was returning home one day, and it dawned on her that except for one brief encounter she had not seen or heard from her friend Brenda Jackson, who only lived two doors down from her. She decided to stop by and visit before Seth and the kids got home. He was picking them up because they both had something after school until five. She had been bringing them home every day since she had started work there, but today she had a little time on her own.

Brenda looked a little surprised when she answered the door. "Are you busy? Am I interrupting anything?" Katie asked.

"No, come on in," Brenda said. "I was on the phone, but I was just finishing when the doorbell rang. Excuse me just a second." As soon as Brenda had hung up the phone, she came back into the living room and explained that she had been talking to her mother.

"I was just on my way home and realized that I had barely seen you since I got back. Did you know I got a job as an aide over at Royal Oaks?"

"Yes, I heard that," said Brenda. "I was kind of surprised that you were able to get back on over there. Julie said that everyone was kind of upset when you left and broke your contract. Don't get me wrong—I'm glad you got the job, just a little surprised."

"Well, they wouldn't let me teach of course, but I talked with Carl and he seemed to believe me when I told him that I would not do anything like that again. Of course it is different with being an aide I guess."

Looking at her friend, Katie remembered the many days they had spent together. When Brenda's husband had died suddenly of a heart attack five years ago, she and Katie were best friends, and for the next two years Katie had done everything she could to help Brenda adjust. She had invited her over at least once a week, called her almost daily and given her a shoulder to cry on numerous times at special holidays and anniversaries. They had kind of grown apart the year before Katie left because Katie felt depressed so much of the time, but she had assumed they would resume their friendship when she moved back home. That did not seem to be happening. She wondered what had been said between Brenda and Seth during her absence. She wondered if Seth had referred to Brenda when he said that "some of the neighbors advised me against taking you back" and comments like that.

"Well, how is the job going?" Brenda was saying. "Julie said you just stay in your room most of the time and she never sees you."

Katie bit back tears. "I guess I have pretty much kept to my room. Miss Patton doesn't go to the lounge much, so I've just kind of taken my cue from her. I'm not hiding, if that's what you're implying," finished Katie.

"Oh, I wasn't implying anything. I was just stating a fact—I mean that's what Julie said. I didn't mean to make you mad. I just think you may as well get in there and show your face. There's no point in acting like you're ashamed. You're not ashamed, are you?"

"Brenda, I'll just be honest with you. I have a lot of guilt over how much I hurt my family by leaving the way I did. Maybe I am ashamed. I hear comments made by thoughtless gossips sometimes when I am walking down the hall. Not one person with whom I worked, including Julie, has come to say hello to me or tell me they're glad I'm back. What would you do? Miss Patton and the kids love and support me in trying to get back to my old self. That's enough for me right now. I don't have much desire to go to the lounge and socialize."

"I'm sorry, Katie. I guess when you left, and Seth and the kids were so devastated, I just allowed myself to be really angry with you. Then Julie and your co-workers, as well as the neighbors around here, were so critical that I forgot about what a good friend you'd been to me. I really need to hear your side of the story. I've never even asked. When Seth told me he had heard from you and that he was going to take you back, I was afraid for him. He had begun to accept that you were gone for good. I don't know what I was thinking. Please forgive me."

"I can't blame you. But you gave me a scare there for a while. I should have known that it wouldn't be that easy to come back home. Home is not just a place. It's a state of mind.

161

I've been here for several weeks now, but I'm not nearly home yet."

"But you will be someday," said Brenda. "You're a good person. I remember the day Jack died. I don't know what I would have done without you. I've missed you." Brenda walked to Katie and gave her a hug.

"I've missed you too. That last year I lived here, I was here only in body, not in spirit. Something was wrong. I just sank deeper into a weird state of mind. I don't know if it was depression or what, but when I finally left, it seemed like my only option. I'll have to tell you about it sometime, but for now, thank you for wanting to understand," said Katie. "I've got to get home and start dinner."

"Thank you for stopping by," said Brenda.

That's one down and at least a dozen more to go, thought Katie. Probably every neighbor on the street had her on their black list. But at least Brenda seemed to want to listen to her and be her friend again. That was a good start.

CHAPTER 17

It had been more than two years since Katie had been out to
Laurel Creek. She felt guilty about that as she drove down the
little narrow road toward Aunt Esther's. Even before she left,
she had seldom visited her aunt during the last five years. She
had gone out there a few times, but had more or less drifted
away. Aunt Esther always acted pleased when Katie came, but
they had little in common, and busy with work and taking care
of family, Katie had just failed to make the effort to go there.
The houses along the road looked about the same as they had
looked for years. A few cows in the pastures here and there, an
old car up on blocks beside a house, a little paint peeling off a
few houses, mostly run-down dwellings inhabited by people
who were not excessively interested in the upkeep of their
property. Here and there she passed a new house which had
been built by the younger generation, but mostly things looked
the same.

Aunt Esther's house was one of the few two story houses
on the road. It sat back off the main road a good ways down a

little lane. The house had been in the family for years, and two smaller houses had been built at an angle across the lane from it—one was Grandma's house, the one Katie had grown up in, now inhabited by Sarah, one of Katie's distant cousins; the other one was where her dad and stepmother had lived when she was young. It was a very small house, and eventually her dad and stepmother had moved into a larger house in town. The little house had burned down a few years after they moved. As Katie turned down the lane, she noticed that the trees were much taller and crowded than she remembered them. She could only see a small section of her aunt's house from the road. She had always loved coming there except during the last year or two before she left. She wasn't sure whether she stopped loving to come because of her depression, or she became depressed because of something that happened when she was out there, but for some reason, she quit enjoying the place. She always hated herself for not visiting Aunt Esther though.

Aunt Esther was out near the old barn that was closer to the house where Katie grew up when Katie arrived. She started back down the path toward the house when she saw Katie drive up. Katie noticed that her aunt looked much older than she remembered her. She walked like an old woman. Getting out of the car, Katie ran to meet her.

"Katie, darling, I'm so glad to see you! How long has it been? Five years?"

"Not that long I hope!" said Katie. She gave her aunt a big hug, and they headed on back toward the house. "What were you doing up there?"

"Oh, I was just feeding the calf that Don and Sarah have," said Esther. "They are over at his mother's today, helping her with her tobacco, so I told them I'd feed the calf."

"Tell me about everybody. Are Don and Sarah doing okay? I haven't seen them for a long time."

"They're well, I guess. Of course Sarah complains all the time, but she's always done that. Just like her mother. I guess it runs in the family. You know their son, Jacob? He came home from Vietnam and he's completely different. Won't even talk to them, never even visits. They don't even know where he is. It worries Sarah to death," Esther said, shaking her head. "But Don, seems like he just accepts it, never says a word. Of course there's really nothing much to say I guess."

"What about Janie, their daughter, does she live around here?" asked Katie.

"No she and her husband moved over to Manchester last fall," said Esther. "Her husband got some kind of road construction job and they just moved over there. I don't think Don and Sarah thought it was a good idea, but of course they had no say in it. Janie has four little kids now, and she has it hard. Her husband just kind of goes from one job to another, and sometimes they can barely pay the rent and utilities. Don has helped them out several times."

As they entered the back door to her house, Esther said, "I just made a fresh pot of coffee. Let's get us a cup and go sit down and visit." Katie waited while she poured the coffee and then followed her into the living room.

"Tell me about you, Katie, how've you been?"

"I'm fine. I've been back a few weeks now, and I have a job, not teaching, but it is at the school."

"And Seth, is he all right?"

"He's fine. It's kind of hard on all of us, especially Samuel," said Katie.

"I've missed you, Katie. I remember when you were a little tiny thing. I played with you almost like a doll. I'd dress you up and pretend you were mine. You were the cutest thing!" Esther gazed into the next room as if she were seeing that little girl.

"I've missed you too. There was a time when I thought the whole world revolved around you. I thought everything you did or said had to be right," Katie said.

"Really? I never knew that," said Esther.

"Oh, yes. You were the queen. Remember that? Something about you being named after Queen Esther in the Bible."

"I always liked to play that up with everyone—'Queen Esther'! I didn't quite understand the story about her in the Bible, but I'd always quote her—I still remember it: 'I will go to the king even though it is against the law. And if I perish, I perish.'"

"I remember that, and although I had no idea what it meant, I thought it was SO FUNNY, and I'd fall in the floor laughing when you said it."

"We were a pair, weren't we, you and I?" said Aunt Esther, laughing. "I loved you too, and thought you could do no wrong."

"I went to visit Mrs. Hopper, an old teacher of mine, the other day, and she was telling me that I talked about you as if you knew everything. She said she never really met you, but that she certainly knew about you!"

"Those were fun days," said Esther.

Katie sat there a moment and then decided to begin the conversation she had been waiting to begin since she arrived.

"Aunt Esther, did anything ever happen to me that was bad when I was little?" As she asked the question, Katie watched her aunt's face.

Aunt Esther showed a moment of something—was it hesitation, recognition, shock? Then she shook her head slowly back and forth. "No, I reckon not. Why?"

Katie knew she had to be careful. The counselor had warned her that if something had happened, her aunt might not be willing to talk about it. "I just wondered. So I was always happy, and well adjusted? I never had any big problems or anything?"

"No, no. You were fine," Esther said, and began immediately to tell a story about something funny that had happened. Katie couldn't put her finger on it, but somehow she thought Esther was holding something back, refusing to talk about something important. Maybe it was just her imagination. She may as well drop it for this visit though, because if she pushed too hard, Esther might just close up for good. She had to leave the door open. Her counselor had advised her not to demand anything, just keep the conversation going until something slipped.

Despite the fact that Katie did not learn anything significant, she enjoyed her visit with Esther and was glad she had gone there. Esther made her promise to come back soon, and Katie assured her that she would.

"Well, how did your visit with your Aunt go last week?" was her counselor's first question.

"Great. I love her. I feel badly that I had let so much time go by without seeing her."

"Did you learn anything that helped you?" he asked.

"Well, yes and no. I did not really learn anything, but unless my mind is playing tricks on me, there is something. She just wouldn't tell what it was. You know how sometimes people just respond in a way that makes you convinced they're hiding something? When I asked Aunt Esther about my childhood, if anything bad had ever happened, I'm certain that just for a moment she remembered something, and then she answered that there was not. But unlike Mrs. Allen and Mrs. Hopper, who just said, 'Not that I know of,' my aunt seemed almost to be trying to convince me that there was nothing. Then she seemed to want to change the subject. I did not push it, but I'm certain that she knows something."

"Katie, you'd be a good detective. You know how to handle people," Dr. Adams said, laughing.

"I don't know about that, but I'm going to keep visiting with Aunt Esther until I get the truth."

Her counseling session went well and Dr. Adams was encouraging about her new job.

It had been nearly three weeks since Katie had visited Aunt Esther, and she had one particular question she wanted to ask her. She and Aunt Esther had walked up to the barn to feed the cow, and Katie was watching Esther as she picked up a pitchfork of hay and threw it over into the stall. Katie glanced around inside the barn and suddenly she felt cold all over and nauseous. She stepped outside the barn, and immediately she felt calmer.

"What's wrong?" asked Esther.

"Nothing, I guess. I just felt kind of sick. It stinks in there," said Katie.

"I'm used to it," said Esther. "You don't notice it after a while. You used to play up here all the time when you were little. I'd miss you and I always knew where you'd be. Usually there were little kittens up here, and I'd find you holding them in your arms."

As they started on back down the path to the house, Katie said, "Esther, you know that little house that my dad used to live in, the one that burned, could you tell me something about it?"

"Sure, I reckon I could," said Esther. "I knew it in every detail. After your dad and Liz moved out, I actually lived in it a few months. I always loved it. It was small, but just cozy enough to be perfect for one person."

"I didn't know that you lived there," said Katie.

"I think it may have been while you were in college. I thought I'd like living by myself. But I didn't of course, and when Mammie got sick, I just moved back in with her. But I did like the little house. I just didn't like being by myself. Now of course, I got no choice, but back then I did. Anyway, what did you want to know about the house?"

"It seems like I remember a tiny little room, but Grandma's house didn't have one. Did that house have a little room off the kitchen, kind of like a laundry room or something?" asked Katie.

"As a matter of fact, it did," said Esther. "I'm not sure what it was meant for originally, but when your dad lived there, he had a washing machine in there, and when I was living there, I had one in there too. Of course when the house was built they had no electricity, or running water, so I don't know what it was used for then. I just remember that when your dad was there he put a washing machine in there and I liked the idea, so I did too. Why did you remember that?"

"I don't know. It just came to me. I just remember that room and the washing machine," she said slowly.

A flicker of something crossed Aunt Esther's wrinkled face quickly and was gone. "Well, that's strange," she responded. "Are you ready to go back inside now?"

"Yes, that's fine. I'd like a glass of water, if you don't mind," said Katie. "And then I'd better be going. Did I tell you I'm working again?"

"Yes, but you didn't tell me how it's going. I hope you're liking it," said her aunt.

"I am. I like it much better than I thought I would. I never thought I'd like working with the primary grades, but they're the sweetest kids, and I love Miss Patton, the teacher I work with."

"That's good. I'm glad for you. I hope you do well there," Aunt Esther said sincerely.

"I think if I could ever figure out why I left my family the way I did, I might be able to get past it, but I just know there's some reason I did that, and until I find out, I'm not sure I can ever really feel secure in who I am and what makes me tick," Katie said.

"Oh, you'll be fine," encouraged Esther. "I just know you will."

"But I'm not sure that my family can be certain that it won't happen again if we don't have any idea what caused it. It's a subject we don't talk about, but it's always there. I told you that I'm going to a counselor. Well, both he and my counselor in Nashville feel that there is something in my past, something that happened to me that somehow was triggered before I left. They think that I have pushed it down and repressed it, but it's still there in my subconscious," said Katie.

170

Esther looked hard at Katie. "I don't understand all those words you're using, Katie, but do you believe them, that something happened to you?"

"I don't really know. Sometimes I do. I have these flashes of pictures in my mind that I don't understand, and I think maybe they're memories of something that happened. It happened up there in the barn a while ago. You know when I felt sick, and we were talking about the smell? Well, I don't really think it was a smell. I think it was a memory of some sort. I know it all sounds crazy, and it may be, but that's what I felt."

Aunt Esther said nothing. She just walked on into the kitchen and got Katie's water, and after handing it to her, went into the living room and sat down. Katie drank some water, then stood and told Aunt Esther she had better get back home.

"I've enjoyed this so much," said Esther. "You come back again—soon."

"Oh, I will," promised Katie. And she meant it.

Both Katie's and Samuel's counseling sessions had been changed to the afternoons since she had started to work, and she had been able to get hers on a different day so that Samuel would not have to wait while she talked to Dr. Adams. She had hoped that she might talk Seth into having the whole family go for a few sessions, but he had remained adamant that he saw no purpose in that, and Abby had seemed to be gradually depending more on her and trusting her more. She felt that she and Seth still had a ways to go though before he really trusted her as she would like him to. She did not know if the counseling would help, but she wished he would give it a try. She could not see any real improvement in Samuel, so it was hard for her to push Seth about them all going. There was one thing about Samuel, though. He was less resistant about going, so he must be seeing some value in it. Or maybe he had just settled into the fact that he had to go. Anyway, when they left for his session on Thursday, he seemed in a fair mood.

"How do you feel about Dr. Adams now, Samuel? I know you did not want to go to him. Is he helping you in any way that you can see?" Katie asked, hoping for at least a civil response.

"He's okay I guess. Mom, he said that sometimes people do weird things like you did because of something that happened to them, and they don't even understand it themselves. Is that true of you? Do you know why you left us?" He said, looking, not at her, but out the window.

"No," she said. "I really don't. I wish I did." Tears were nearly filling her eyes and she could say no more.

"Well, it just sounds like a lot of bull to me," he said. "I think it's just an excuse for not taking responsibility for your actions."

"I can understand why you'd feel that way. I'd probably feel the same way if I were in your shoes," she said. "I wish it had never happened, but I can't take that back."

Samuel seemed to consider the conversation over, and she did not bring it up again. He seemed so mature in some ways, and in other ways he still seemed just like a little boy. He was actually doing quite well in school this year, and his teachers all said that his scores in both math and reading had improved greatly.

She tried to get out to talk to Aunt Esther once a week, but she realized that it had been about three weeks since she had been there. With work, the counseling sessions, and helping the kids with homework, it was just impossible to get out there during the week, so she had to resort to weekends when Seth could be around to supervise the children. Sunday afternoons were usually the only times she could manage to get out there.

"I was hoping you'd come this afternoon," Aunt Esther said, hugging her. "I've been here by myself all week. Don and Sarah have gone to see Sarah's grandmother, who is very sick, and I'm used to having them to talk with. I think they were gone the last time you were here. Seems like they are always going off somewhere for a few days. Anyway, come on in. I just made a fresh apple cake. Want a piece? It's still hot!"

"How could I refuse? I can't even refuse your apple cake when it's a day old, but still warm, it'll be delicious," said Katie.

Esther went to the kitchen followed by Katie, who sat down at the kitchen table. Esther cut a piece of cake and then went to the refrigerator and poured a glass of cold milk. Katie ate the cake eagerly. "That's the best, Aunt Esther!" she said.

"I'm glad you enjoyed it. There's nothing like a piece of warm cake. I ate a piece as soon as I got it out of the oven. How're things with you? It's been a few weeks since you've been here. Been busy, I guess," she said.

"I have been very busy, and I'm sorry I've not been here. Since I started working, it seems like there's always something," Katie lamented. "But I've wanted to come, I really have."

"How have you and Seth and the kids been doing? I mean, do you think you're making good progress getting healthy again—know what I mean?" asked Esther. Katie sensed that her aunt was very concerned about her.

"I don't know, Aunt Esther. I think we're doing okay, but I may just have to give up on trying to find out why I left. Maybe it's just not possible. By the way, did I ever tell you about the morning I left—what actually sent me into a panic that made me feel like I had to run for my life?" Katie asked.

"No. I don't think so. You said you'd been depressed for a long time. And then you said something the last time about having flashes of memories that made no sense. But I don't remember anything specific," Aunt Esther said. "What happened?"

"Well, as I said, I'd been depressed for a long time, and had got the feeling, probably because I was depressed, that Seth didn't appreciate me and thought I was a poor mother. I guess I was rather paranoid, but I had the idea that Seth just didn't approve of me. He had gotten rather critical at times, but when I look back on it, I feel that his criticism was not as severe as it seemed at the time. Anyway, on the morning of the day I left, what sent me over the edge doesn't make a lot of sense, but this is what happened." Katie related to her aunt the story of how she had panicked when she realized that Seth's shirts were covered in the reddish-brown water. She mentioned that at that time she remembered the little room in the house where her dad had lived.

Aunt Esther listened carefully, shaking her head back and forth. She looked as if she were about to say something, and then didn't. Finally, she said, "And now you realize that Seth really wasn't meaning to be that critical? So you …it was probably just that you were so depressed that you thought he was being critical. Right?"

"Yes, I guess so. But why would I have had such a strange reaction to what happened with the shirts? The counselors, both of them, attached a lot of significance to that. You don't think that's important?"

"Honey, I don't know. I guess it could be, but what could have happened to you in the laundry room? I know your grandmother was never particular about laundry. I don't know if you even ever helped her wash. And anyway she washed outdoors most of the time. So, you see, it just makes no sense, does it?" Katie thought that Esther was trying too hard to dismiss the idea that something significant happened in the laundry room. She seemed upset at the idea, and as she talked, Katie realized that although she would not give up trying, she was probably not going to learn anything from Aunt Esther today. Dr. Adams was right. It would take longer to get Esther to give up her secrets. She decided to change the subject to something more pleasant and forget the past for now.

CHAPTER 18

As her friendship with Brenda was rekindled, Katie realized how complicated the relationship was with so many people. Seth had gotten the sympathy with so many people who had come to his aid in the community during those first few months, and those people were not so willing to welcome her back with open arms. Although Seth was now much more understanding because they had talked through so many things while she was still in Nashville, and then he had seen her beaten and bruised from Kirk's attack, so he had time to renew his relationship with her. But the community and her coworkers had not had that, so they still more or less hated her for leaving him. She would have to prove herself to them, just as she had had to do with Seth, but it wouldn't be as simple, because she seldom saw them.

"Maybe we could have a town hall meeting, and you could speak to all them at once," laughed Brenda. "You know, answer all their questions at once. Advertise it as 'all you ever wanted to know about my running away.'"

"That's not funny," said Katie, but she laughed anyway. It was good for her to have a friend to talk to about the whole situation.

At home, she was beginning to feel that things were some better, especially with Abby, but she felt that until she could find out what had happened in her childhood, which she was sure something had, she could never be wholly back home with the love and trust of both Samuel and Seth. She knew that Seth loved her and wanted to believe in her, but she didn't see either he or Samuel could ever forgive her without some answers. She had a chance of mending her relationship with Abby, but she too would probably be scarred by the experience for life, even though she would not necessarily blame her mother.

One day Brenda had stopped by for a visit while Seth and the kids were at a ball game, and Katie was talking to her about her belief that something had happened in her childhood which had left an indelible scar, but which she had completely forgotten.

"Can you do that? Just forget something completely?" asked Brenda.

"They say that you can. But it's still there in your subconscious, and it can resurface if there's something to trigger the memory," said Katie.

"That's really strange," said Brenda "So do you have any idea what it was?"

"Not really," Katie said, and then told her about the washing machine incident.

"Why don't you ask your aunt? Wouldn't she know?"

"Maybe, but if she does, she won't tell," said Katie. "I've tried to ask her, and I actually think she knows something, but she won't say anything."

"Maybe she did something, so she doesn't want you to know it," said Brenda.

"No, I don't think so," said Katie. "It's not like that. I can't explain it, but I'm sure she was not involved. Anyway, she was young herself when this must have happened, only twelve or fourteen. But I think she knows something, even if she doesn't know it all."

"You said you lived with your grandmother as a child, right?" Brenda asked.

"Yes, but she's been dead several years. My Aunt Esther is my great-aunt, my grandmother's youngest sister."

"What about your dad? Why didn't you live with him?" asked Brenda.

"I don't know. He and my step-mom lived next door at first and later moved into London, but I always lived with Grandma," Katie said.

"What about your mother? Didn't you say that your mom and dad were divorced? Where is she?" asked Brenda.

"To be honest I have no idea where she is. She left us when I was a baby, and that's about all I know, except that her name was Ora Mae—strange name—and I don't even know what her last name is now, or where she lives. When I was little I asked a few questions about her, and the only thing Grandma would say was 'You don't want to be like her.'"

"Isn't that rather odd, you living with your grandma, and your dad living next door?" For the first time Katie realized she had never questioned that, just accepted it as normal.

"Maybe what happened to you is connected to why you lived with Grandma. Did you ever think about it that way?" said Brenda.

"No I never did," said Katie, "but you're right. That would be a good question to ask Aunt Esther.

CHAPTER 19

When she hung up the phone, Ora Mae Fields could not believe someone from the Royal family had actually called. Many years ago both Ed and his mother had told her they never wanted to talk to her again, and she had never gone back. She had often wondered how her baby girl had grown up, what kind of person she was. It was ironic that her former husband's last name was Royal, because that was how she had always thought of them. Compared to her own upbringing, Ed's family lived like "royalty." They weren't rich by most standards, but they acted like they were better than everybody else. Compared to her family, of course, they were rich. Her family had barely enough to eat from day to day, and once or twice they had actually had to live in an old barn for a few days. Her dad never could hold a job because of his drinking, and her mo ther was always sick. When she was fifteen, they sent her to live with her aunt, who never really wanted to be bothered with her. She ran with a wild crowd and did whatever she wanted to, because the main thing her aunt cared about was not having to be bothered with her.

Not long after she went to live with her aunt, she met Ed Royal. She was crazy about him. He was handsome, quiet, and he seemed genuinely interested in her. Soon he took her to his home, which was so much different than she had ever seen. They not only had a nice home, but their farm was huge, and you could tell they never wanted for anything to eat or wear, and they certainly never had to worry about where they would sleep at night.

Ora Mae was not so much in love with Ed, but with his way of life. She thought she'd get around to loving him later. Despite the fact that she could tell his folks were not in favor of it, she and Ed married less than a year later. They moved into a small cottage located on the Royal property, just across the road from Ed's mother. His father had died a few years before and she lived there with her younger son, Rufus. Her mother-in-law was a pleasant enough woman, but Ora Mae knew that she thought Ed had married beneath him. At first, she tried to please the family, but except for Rufus, who was always friendly and tried to make her feel welcome, and Ed's Aunt Esther, who was just a teenager herself, they never made her feel a part of the family. It was nothing big, just little things. For example, Ed's mother and grandmother, who also lived next door, would sometimes stop talking when she came into the room, and it was obvious to her that she had been the topic of conversation. And when a question was asked, if Ora Mae ventured to answer it, they would then ask someone else, as if her answer had not been given.

Unfortunately perhaps, for Ora Mae, she became pregnant almost immediately. While all the rest of the family seemed ecstatic over this development, she was scared to death. She was so young, and she knew nothing about babies. Before she had met Ed, she had just begun to enjoy the attention of several young men and to be proud of the way her body seemed to attract them. When she met Ed, he was of course attracted to her and she enjoyed that. But pregnancy began to destroy that image of herself, and she hated it. Nevertheless, when the little squalling baby came, she couldn't help but fall in love with her. She spent hours playing with her, dressing her up in the cute little dresses that Ed's mother made her.

For a young immature girl like Ora Mae though, motherhood had a devastating effect. Her stomach still looked big, her breasts stayed engorged during breast feeding, she got very little sleep, and Ed didn't pay much attention to her now that she was a mother. It seemed like he was always out working on the farm or over at his mother's visiting with his family. She began to crave companionship, and she knew that she had to work on the way she looked. Most of the clothes she had worn before baby Katherine was born did not fit. She asked Ed to take her into town to shop for some clothes, and he did. She was a size larger, but the clothes she bought boosted her feelings about herself, and she began to plan a way to get out and meet some new people. She remembered seeing a girl she knew at the store where she bought her dresses. She was able to get a ride into town with Rufus the next day. She went by the store and talked to the girl.

"I am suffocating from motherhood!" said Ora Mae.

"I've got the cure for that," said her friend. "Come back here." Ora Mae followed her to the back of the store where the girl opened her purse and pulled out a bottle of whiskey.

"Where did you get that?" asked Ora Mae.

"Do you remember Johnny? He knows my mother won't let me drink, so he brings me some once in a while." They both laughed at memories of Johnny, took a few drinks of the whiskey and Ora Mae was getting ready to leave.

"If you're tired of all the family responsibility, why don't you come down to Johnny's tonight? We go there every Thursday and hang out a while, like you did before you met your 'Royal' husband." Said her friend.

"Oh, I couldn't. I don't even have a way to go anywhere," Ora Mae admitted.

"No problem. I'll pick you up at seven. Just be ready."

"I'll try. But I'll have to ask Ed. He'll have to stay with little Katherine," said Ora Mae.

At first Ed was against her going, but when she said a girlfriend was picking her up and she would not be late, he agreed that maybe she needed a break. That was the beginning of the end for Ed and Ora Mae's marriage. The first few nights she went out she came back by midnight. Then it got to be two or three. Then it was morning, and then sometimes noon the next day. Ora Mae spent the nights here and there, mostly with both men and women, but sometimes just men. She began to stay out several nights at a time. Ed would become angry, but sometimes she felt that he was covering up for her with his mother, because he did not want to admit to his family that his wife was behaving in such a way. Then when she was gone for several days, he had to get help with the baby, so he had to make up stories, and finally he must have told them the truth.

Eventually Ed gave her an ultimatum: either she stay at home and stop going out at night or she would have to leave. He made it plain that she would be leaving without baby Katherine. She began to cry and promised him that she would stay. Unfortunately, Ora Mae was in too deep by then. She was beginning to crave the alcohol, and she felt stifled by life at home. One night about ten o'clock, she heard a faint knock on her window and it was Jason Olson, one of the young men she had been spending a lot of time with the last few months. She raised the window and chatted with him. He begged her to come with him, saying that they would run away, make a good life and eventually send for her baby. Although her logic told her that Ed and his mother would never permit that, her emotions allowed her to believe the lie. She planned her escape for the next night, packed a few things and met Jason at the end of the lane, never returning.

The next day, true to his promise, Jason took Ora Mae with him as he traveled north to Ohio. The first few weeks were like a honeymoon for Ora Mae. She missed baby Katherine more than she had expected though, and she called home to check on her.

Ed answered as soon as the phone rang. When he heard her voice, he just said, "Ora Mae, don't be calling here again. I want nothing to do with you."

"But Katherine..." she began. Hearing the dial tone, she knew she would not be heard.

Another time she tried calling home, and Ed's mother answered the phone. "Mrs. Royal, I just wanted to ask about my baby..." she began, when she was interrupted.

"You don't have a baby daughter any more, Ora Mae. You ran away from her, so don't call back." As she hung up, Jason came up from behind her.

"Ora Mae, I'm going to have to ask you not to be calling home again," he said sharply. "We don't have that kind of money."

That was the first of many more times when Jason showed his controlling nature, the nature which Ora Mae had not seen in him before she left Kentucky. It was seven more years before she was able to tear herself away from him and try to figure out who she really wanted to be. By then she knew that trying to go backward in time was useless. She could only go forward. Working in a factory in Dayton, Ohio, she met a man with whom she was able to share all the details of her life. They eventually married and moved to Detroit, where he was promised a job. Al was kind and supportive, leaving her to make all her decisions about how to live her life. She felt that had they not been so far away from Kentucky, he would have supported her in trying to figure out a way to reconnect with her daughter. Unfortunately, Al and Ora Mae lived a life almost as meager as the one she had lived before meeting Ed. They often could not meet their routine obligations for rent, utilities, and groceries, and seldom had money enough to get medical care when they were sick, which Ora Mae often was. They had a happy life together though, and she continued to work all she could and eventually was put on a good insurance plan at work.

When Al died suddenly of a heart attack at age sixty, Ora Mae was devastated. Soon afterward, she received word that Al had paid into a life insurance plan for all the years that they had been married, the result of which was enough for her to live more comfortably than she had ever lived before. She considered it a blessing, although for her part, she would have preferred to have had Al than any amount of money.

Nevertheless, when Esther Royal called, saying that her daughter had had a rough year, and she thought it might be a help in her healing to meet her mother after all these years, Ora Mae started making plans to drive to Kentucky.

CHAPTER 20

"What is wrong with my father? What happened to him?"

Seth looked at Katie, sighed, and then said, "Who knows? If I remember correctly, it started right after you left. First, Aunt Esther said he wouldn't go anywhere for several weeks and she didn't think he was eating. Then she talked about him sleeping all the time."

"Sounds like depression, doesn't it?" Katie said.

"I guess. Anyway, after a while they took him to the doctor, and he seemed to do a little better for a few weeks, then....I just really don't remember too much about it. I had my own worries." Seth cleared his throat. "Anyway, he just basically withdrew into himself to the point that they didn't feel it was safe for him to live over there alone. He's been in the nursing home in Corbin for about a year now I guess. Sometimes Esther or someone goes to visit him, but they say most of the time, he's lying in his bed and doesn't talk to them, or if he does, it doesn't make much sense."

"Do you think I should go visit him?" Katie asked.

"Well, it couldn't hurt, but don't assume he'll talk to you."

"The more I think about it, the more I think there's something strange about my relationship to him, Seth. He's my dad, but he never really seemed like my dad when I was growing up. I mean, I saw him a lot, but I didn't ever stay with him and Liz, or really depend on him for anything. Doesn't that seem odd to you?"

"Yes, it does. Did he buy you things or take you places? Well, he did occasionally buy me things, but he never took me anywhere that I remember. I always got the feeling that Grandma Royal wouldn't have let me go. I don't remember why."

"Was he good to you?"

"He was always kind to me, never criticized me, even when I misbehaved. Sometimes I'd notice him staring at me in a sad kind of way, like he regretted something. Most of the time, though, he was pleasant enough." Katie stood, ending the conversation. "I'll have to go see him."

"I guess so. You want to go tomorrow? I'll get the kids or whatever needs to be done."

Driving to Corbin that morning Katie made a mental list of things she needed to ask Ed Royal. She knew that he would probably not answer her, but she needed to be ready, just in case. When she pulled up to the Southeast Healthcare Center, she grabbed the small yellow notepad on which she had written the address of the facility, and added some of her questions so she would not forget them. The large sign in front of the one story brick building was surrounded by pink and white azalea bushes in full bloom and the lawn looked well-kept. Hesitating for a moment to look in the mirror, Katie took a deep breath, picked up her purse, got out of the car, and walked slowly toward the door marked "ENTRANCE."

Before she reached the door, she stopped briefly to look down at her notes, and at the exact time, an older lady in a white uniform, opened the door. "Come on in, honey. We love visitors around here."

"Oh, thank you, Miss…"

"I'm Betty. Who are you visiting? I can take you right to the room. I've been working here so long I know everybody."

"Ed Royal. I'm here to visit him."

"Ed Royal? Now that's a new one. No one ever comes to visit him. And even when his aunt does occasionally come, he won't talk to her. Who are you? A relative?"

"I'm his daughter."

The woman looked stunned. "He has a daughter? I didn't know he had a daughter. Why have you not visited before?" She suddenly stopped and covered her mouth in embarrassment. "I'm sorry. I didn't mean to be critical. You don't have to answer that. I'm sure you have your reasons. I'm just shocked to learn he has a daughter."

"That's okay. I've been living out of town. It's a long story, but anyway, now I'm here. Can you tell me a little about his condition? I don't quite know what to expect."

"Sure. Your father came to us close to a year ago. The doctor said he had extreme depression and maybe some dementia, short-term memory loss, that kind of thing. As I said, he seldom has visitors, and when he does he often refuses to talk to them. He takes his meals in the dining room, but he usually sits alone and I've never seen him talking to anyone much. I'll be glad to take you to see him. I don't know how he'll react though. The last time his aunt Esther came, he was lying on his bed, and he just turned over with his face to the wall when she came in."

"Thank you so much, Betty. Now I'd like you to take me to his room if you don't mind."

"Sure. Right this way."

Katie's feet felt like clay as she walked down the long hall. She breathed heavily and her hands were ice cold. Betty walked ahead of her and knocked briefly and then opened the door.

"Mr. Royal, you have a visitor! It's your lucky day!"

Katie entered behind her to see the shadow of a man she used to know seated in a padded rocking chair, moving slightly back and forth. He stopped his rocking back and forth for a moment, stared at her, and then began rocking back and forth again. In the moment of stillness though, Katie was almost sure there was recognition.

"What do you want?" he asked, no expression showing on his face.

"It's Katie, Papa," she said, using the name she called him as a child. Out of the corner of her eye she saw Betty politely nod to her and exit the room so they could visit privately.

Ed Royal, stopped his chair again, and looked toward the floor. "You're not dead then?" he said.

"No, of course not, Papa. I've been living in Nashville for about two years, but I've come back home, now. I didn't know you were here until I came back home."

"And your arm? Is it better now?"

What an odd question. "Oh yes, Papa, it's fine."

"Liz died, you know, she didn't leave me purposely. She had cancer." Katie remembered how devastated her father had been at Liz's funeral several years ago.

"Yes, I know. You still miss her I'm sure."

190

"I do miss her, but I wish you could have stayed too. I loved you, you know."

"Do you mean I couldn't live with you because you married Liz?" Now maybe she was going to get some answers.

Suddenly Ed Royal began fumbling with the chair arm and rose from the chair. "I'm sorry, but I'm very tired and must take a nap," he said. Simultaneously holding the chair arm and the side of his bed he managed to get seated on his small bed and lay back on his pillow. "Who did you say you were?" He asked.

"Papa, it's me, Katie. Remember?"

As he turned over toward the wall, Ed Royal said distinctly, "Mom said no one was going to jail."

Katie stood shocked for a few moments, then she realized that the conversation was over, at least for this visit.

CHAPTER 21

"Katie, how good to see you again," Aunt Esther said, hugging her tightly. "How are the kids? And Seth? Is he doing well?"

"They're fine," said Katie. "All of them are fine. I wouldn't say that it's perfect, but I've made some progress with Samuel, and Abby is doing great in school. Actually Samuel's grades were much better this grading period too, which may be due to the fact that he and I are beginning to make progress. I actually helped with a book report last week and he seemed to appreciate it."

"Well, good. What brings you out this way? Don't tell me you just came to visit. I know better. You're always looking for something. What is it this time?"

"Aunt Esther, I went to visit Dad last week." For just a moment, her aunt looked as if she had seen a ghost, like she was really scared, but she blinked and then regained her composure.

"I'm sorry, Aunt Esther. I know that you get tired of all my questions. But the fact is, I am convinced that something happened to me that was very traumatic when I was little. I have also come to believe that my life cannot be as it should be until I find out what it was and deal with it. It's true that my family and I are plugging along pretty well now. But I think it's all patching up wounds, trying to deal with them, but not really allowing them to heal. As long as I don't know what happened, I always worry that something will trigger my subconscious again and I might do something completely irrational. And I think Seth and the kids feel the same way."

"I've been thinking about that since you were here the last time, and I worry about it too. I have decided that no matter what happens, I have to tell you the truth. It has been weighing on my heart ever since you came back. I decided I have to live up to my name. I am Esther, so I have to do what's right, no matter the cost. So what did you want to know."

"I wanted to talk to you about my parents. Why did I live with Grandma and not my dad and stepmother?"

"Well, it's rather complicated," said the old woman, looking down at her hands. "Sis, your grandma, swore me to secrecy. She said that I must never tell anyone, not even you. She said it would kill your dad if you ever found out."

"Well, Grandma Royal is dead now. And I visited my father in the nursing home the other day. He seemed so confused. At one time he asked who I was, and he said some rather weird things."

"I know, but Sis said that I was never to tell. And I tried to do what she said, but the more I talk to you, the more I realize that you have to know the truth about yourself. It'll hurt though, and you may be sorry you even asked. I was young, twelve or fourteen maybe, when it happened." Aunt Esther looked at Katie "Do you remember anything about your arm?"

"What are you talking about?" Katie suspected that Aunt Esther had become confused about the issue they were discussing. "What does my arm have to do with why I didn't live with Dad?"

"I'm talking about why your arm is disfigured and weak. Do you remember anything about why it is that way?" asked Aunt Esther, looking at her closely as if to be sure she would tell the truth.

"I fell into the dirt near the plow. The horse got scared, and stepped on my arm," Katie said, repeating a story she had told ever since she could remember.

"What if I told you that that is not how your arm was hurt?" said Esther. "What if I told you that there was another story, explaining your injuries? One which is connected to why you always lived with Sis."

Katie stared at the old woman. What was she saying? None of this made any sense. She could see herself falling and being trampled by the horse. She didn't exactly remember it, but it was her reality, the only one she had ever known. How could her injuries have anything to do with why she lived with Grandma?

"I don't understand," she said. "What do you mean? Tell me. Tell me everything." Her aunt rocked back and forth for several minutes before she began her story. She seemed to be trying to decide where to start and at the same time whether she should tell the story at all or not. It had been stored up for a long time, forbidden by her older sister, who had really been like a mother to her.

Finally she looked up at the ceiling and said, "Sis, I'm sorry, but I have to tell Katie this. It's important that she understand. Please forgive me." She then looked at Katie and said, "Katie, I have to tell you some things that may be painful for you, and I'm sorry. You are a good person and you have a wonderful husband and family. If you know the truth, maybe you can turn it into something beautiful that will help your family become all God intended it to be."

Katie sat very still and stared at the tired-looking old woman. "I have no idea what you're talking about."

" I'll just have to start at the beginning, which was when you were born. Your mother was not a bad person, but she was not ready for marriage and a family when you were born. She was very young. I remember she did not seem much older than I was. Soon after you came along, she started disappearing for a day or two at a time. I never knew where she was or what she was doing during those times. I'm not sure that your dad did either. Your uncle Rufus, he was a little younger than your dad, still lived at home and he would sometimes make remarks about your mother, but Sis would usually tell him to keep quiet. Rufus was very different from your dad. Your dad was quiet; Rufus was loud. Your dad was serious; Rufus was all about having a good time. I loved going over there, mainly because Rufus was so much fun. Your dad would bring you over to Sis's place once in a while and say, 'Ora Mae's gone, Mom. Could you keep Katie today?' And of course your grandma would always say yes. Sometimes when I was there, I'd see a look pass between them, but nothing much was said.

"Eventually I learned that your mother was seeing other men, and finally she moved out and we never heard from her again. I always liked your mom and always wondered where she went, but I never asked much about her, because when I did, I could tell it made both your dad and your grandma mad to have anyone mention her. Anyway, your dad finally made the divorce official, and moved on with his life, living over there with you. He had a girl come in during the day to take care of you while he worked and sometimes he'd bring you over to Sis's house on weekends or in the evenings. The houses—my parent's, Sis's, and the little cottage where you and your dad lived were all very close, so there was a lot of going back and forth all the time.

"About two or three years after your mother left, someone told me that your dad had a new girlfriend. Over the next few months we got to know Liz, as she too, was often at Sis's house as well as yours and mine. Anyway, Uncle Rufus teased her a lot, and I could tell that your dad did not like Rufus to be around much. At the time, I wondered what the problem was, but later I realized that it was jealousy of his brother's ability to be comfortable around everyone and have a good time. I think the experience with your mother played into it too. He was scared of losing Liz. I don't know that there was ever anything really between Rufus and Liz, but they did talk a lot and over a series of weeks, it was obvious to all of us that your dad resented Rufus' presence around the house. One day when I was at Sis's house, Rufus started to leave, and Sis asked him where he was going.

'Over to Ed's, to get a saddle,' he said.

'I think you'd better stay away a while, Rufus,' said Sis.

'Oh I'm just going to the barn,' he said.

'Well, you stay away from Liz,' said Sis.

'Liz is not over there,' he said.

"When he left I went out to the garden to get pick some beans. While I was out there I noticed that Liz came down the road and stopped briefly as if listening and then went on into the barn. I never thought any more about it, and later in the morning went on back to my house.

"In the late afternoon I heard a big commotion over at Sis's, and ran over there. There were several people, including the sheriff, over at Ed's. We learned that Rufus had been shot inside the barn and was dead. No one knew where Ed was, and they were looking for him. The girl who had been keeping you that afternoon said that he had brought you over to her house that morning and asked her to take you back home. She did, but she did not know where Ed was or anything about the murder. Later in the evening, the Sheriff found Ed and questioned him, but of course Ed said he knew nothing about the shooting—that he had left that morning. Back then the police did little unless someone pressed charges, and no one did."

"But how does this explain why I lived with Grandma?" asked Katie.

"I'm getting to that," said her aunt. "The next day I was over at Sis's house, and the girl who had come to watch you came running over there and said that Sis must come quickly, your dad was hurting you. Sis ran out with her and was gone for a while. When she returned, she was holding you in her arms and soothing you. You were badly bruised and obviously beaten, your arm looking like it had been broken. Your grandmother did not call a doctor, but set the arm herself and coddled you for days, cooing and worrying over you. She barely left you long enough to go to Rufus's funeral."

"So I guess that's why Papa asked me if my arm was okay."

"He said that?"

"Yes. He first said, 'Then you're not dead?' Then he said, 'And your arm—is it all right?' I couldn't figure why he said those things."

Esther said, "Later Sis told me that you had found some of your dad's bloody clothes in a small room off the kitchen and that you had apparently told your dad that you were washing the clothes he had had on when he shot Uncle Rufus. I got the impression that maybe you had seen or your father thought you'd seen him shoot Rufus. When your grandmother found the two of you, he was yelling at you that you were never to say he killed uncle Rufus, and he was beating you. Your grandma apparently grabbed him and almost gave him a beating. She finally agreed not to report him if he agreed to let her raise you and never interfere, an agreement which I reckon he kept."

"But why did I think a horse stepped on me?" asked Katie.

"I don't remember exactly how that happened, but I think that when people asked Sis what happened to you, which of course they would, she just told them that you were stepped on by a horse because you were playing close to the plow, and fell. No one questioned it, or at least not openly, so it just became reality for everyone, including you. I guess you just blocked out what really happened."

"And Liz just went on and married him? Did she know who shot Uncle Rufus?"

"She must have, but it was never talked about openly," said Aunt Esther. "I always thought that she might have been in the barn with Rufus, and your dad caught them. Even if it was an innocent meeting, she probably felt responsible. Or at least that's what I thought."

"What about his hurting me? Did she know why my Grandma raised me?"

"I think she had to have known, but if she did, she never mentioned it to my knowledge. Sis never told anyone."

"So Grandma just let my dad get by with killing his brother and nearly ruining my arm? Just never made him accountable?"

"She was devastated of course, losing one son already. She just couldn't bring herself to make your dad face the consequences of his actions. I'm sure there were many speculations about all of it in the community, but no one knew for sure, except Sis. The girl who had been keeping you when this happened just kind of disappeared. I don't know what happened to her. She may have known more than we realized, but I never knew what she did with the information."

"This explains a lot. It explains why I panicked when I saw the laundry being ruined. In my mind I must have connected my fear that Seth would be mad about his shirts being ruined with my dad's anger when he saw me trying to wash the clothes he had ruined with the blood of his brother."

"I'm sorry, Katie," said Aunt Esther. "All that trauma on a little girl. I guess you just pushed it down inside you all those years. But it never left, and somehow it had to come out. Maybe it was beginning to come out that year before you left. It was pushing to be recognized, but you couldn't acknowledge it, so you became very sad instead. I want you to be well, Katie, to be happy again."

"I've just found out that my dad is a murderer and a child beater and that is supposed to make me happy?" Katie asked, tears streaming down her face.

"Katie, your father made some terrible mistakes, but you need to know that he did love you. He never forgave himself for what he did," said Esther. "His actions caused one whole generation of grief. Sis, your dad, me, none of us could ever get past it. And you appeared to have forgotten it, but it was still there in your mind. The only way you can ever heal is to turn loose of it, put it behind you. Your grandma was never able to do that, but you can. You can forgive your dad and move on and make it up to your children. If you hold on to it, you can never be the mother you want to be."

"But I always thought my dad was a good man. I never questioned his character in any way," said Katie. "I feel totally deceived by him. I never got to express anger for something he did to me, and now he is so confused that I'm not sure he'd understand what I was talking about. And Uncle Rufus, he didn't deserve to die. You said yourself that he was a fun-loving person."

"Yes, I know Katie. I hated your father for quite some time. I had always loved both Ed and Rufus. They were my nephews, but since Sis was so much older, they were both older than I was. Rufus always teased me, calling me 'aunt' in a mocking way, just kidding me. And your dad, well, he was always the serious one, but I loved him too. After Rufus died, I was never the happy-go-lucky young girl I was before. I had a hard time coming to this, but I think I finally forgave your father just after he got sick. Mostly I was able to forgive him because he tried so hard. He never complained, even when Sis said some hateful things to him. I had felt pity for him when Liz was diagnosed with cancer, but I must admit that I also felt that it was a kind of justice. Your father was very aware of what terrible things he had done. He became so pitiful, especially after you left. I just couldn't go on holding that anger in me.

201

Sis held it there until she died I think. She was pleasant and loving to you and to me, but she never really forgave Ed."

"But how can you excuse what he did?"

"I don't. I didn't excuse it. I just accepted that he had made some terrible mistakes, but that I still love him and wish him well. The problem is that I don't think he can forgive himself, and it's destroying him. I don't think I can help him do that, but at least I'm at peace with myself and hold no ill will against him."

"I'm sure that's a good thing to do, Aunt Esther. I just don't know if I can do it. I've got to go now, but I'll see you soon."

Katie contained her tears until she pulled out of the driveway at Aunt Esther's, but before she got to the main road, she felt nauseated and had to pull over into a little lane that led up toward one of the pastures. She stopped the car and opened the door and the tears started.

The pieces of the puzzle definitely fit neatly in place now, but to say that the knowledge could lead to happiness for her—that would be a big stretch. Her heart was heavy and she began to remember bits and pieces of conversations that made little sense when she had heard them, but now were crystal clear. She remembered once when she had come home from school and her dad was sitting in the kitchen with her and Grandma. They were sampling the cookies Grandma had just taken out of the oven. Katie was really angry at a friend, and she was railing against her, saying she would like to slap her face. Grandma said, "She's got a temper just like you used to have when you were a kid, Ed."

Her dad spoke up and said, "Girl, you need to work on that, keep that under control. A bad temper can ruin your life forever." Grandma did not respond, and Katie felt that there was an understanding between them that she did not grasp.

Her aunt had said that she needed to forgive to move on with her life and be the kind of mother she wanted to be, and she guessed that was true. But how does one forgive one who has lost the ability to carry on a sensible conversation? That stops in the middle of the conversation and asks who you are? Why did she not demand to know why she couldn't live with her father while she was a child? As she thought about this, she realized that she had actually had a happy childhood. That was more than many children had. But she was so angry with her father for pretending to be something he wasn't. Or had he? He really had never said anything to indicate that he had any rights to her, never disciplined her in any way, or told Grandma what to do. He had kept his promise not to interfere with her life in any way. Her mind kept going back and forth between being his prosecutor and his defender.

In the middle of her musings she heard Samuel's voice saying, "At least I didn't leave, like you did!" Suddenly she realized that she had needed and still needed forgiveness. Maybe her sin had not been as bad in her eyes as her dad's, but she had caused her family much grief, just as her dad had caused his much grief. She had been protected from the hurt as a child, but Abby and Samuel had been exposed to it. If she held on to the anger at her father, what good would it do anyone? It would not bring Rufus back. It would not heal her arm that sometimes still caused her some pain. On the other hand, if she could forgive him, it might make it easier for her own family to forgive her.

She thought about her own mother, and how she had often wondered where she was and why she left her baby girl. She had always tried not to dwell on that because she thought it would make Grandma feel bad to think that Katie really wanted her own mother, but she used to think what it would be like if her mother just showed up one day and took her away, maybe to a very different life in the city. She had forgotten all about all those times she had speculated about what that would be like. She had thought about her mother a lot when she was about Samuel's age.

As Katie sat there she thought back over the many questions that had gone through her mind at different times during her childhood, but which she had put behind her as an adult. She had wanted her own family to be ideal, but she had never really sought to analyze her childhood, or openly question why it was the way it was. Once she was grown, she had never tried to find her mother or even wonder about where she was. In light of all she had learned about her family, her mother's disappearance seemed more interesting now, but not necessarily a tragedy.

It seemed as if Katie had sat there for at least forty-five minutes or an hour, when she finally realized where she was and what time it was. She needed to be home soon. She closed the car door, and backed into the lane to head home.

CHAPTER 22

When Katie got home she was thankful that Seth seemed to understand that she had learned something important from Aunt Esther, and that it was not something she could discuss with him until the kids were off to bed. He probably could see the obvious signs that she had been crying. He gave her a hug and allowed her to take her time in deciding when it was time to talk. She went straight to the kitchen and began to prepare dinner, taking time to speak to the kids about homework and chores that needed to be done.

"Mom, will you help me make a poster for my book report?" asked Samuel.

"Of course," answered Katie. Such a routine request might have meant little to most mothers. They might have even been burdened by it. But for Katie, she was so happy she almost cried for joy. Even if he was just using her, it was a start. It made her forget momentarily the feelings she had as a result of learning the truth about her father. She hummed a pleasant tune as she finished browning the ground beef to make spaghetti sauce and got the rolls ready for the oven.

It was late by the time dinner was over, the dishes were put away, and Samuel leaned his poster proudly against the back of the couch. "Look, Dad, don't you think this is an awesome poster?"

"Yes, as a matter of fact, I do," said Seth. "I would have never thought of using the construction paper cut-outs like that."

"That was Mom's idea," said Samuel. "I wouldn't have thought of it either, but it does look neat. I think my English teacher will love it."

"Good. Don't forget to lay out your clothes for school tomorrow. You have pictures tomorrow, remember," said his dad.

"Actually, Mom has already hung my shirt on my door. She had to iron it, so we decided to leave it out. Good night, Dad," Samuel said as he bounded up the stairs. It was obvious that Samuel had begun to forgive Katie and accept her back into his life.

Katie had gone up a few minutes before and helped Abby get ready for bed and pick out clothes for school tomorrow. She came down the stairs with an armload of clothes to put in the washing machine. She went into the laundry room and loaded the clothes in the washer, and came out closing the door.

"Katie, come and sit beside me. I know that you learned something today. Want to talk about it?" Seth asked.

Katie dropped down on the couch as if under a heavy weight. As Seth put an arm around her, she burst into tears for the first time since she had returned home. She thought she had cried it all out when she had pulled off the little lane leading up to her old home place, but now, with Seth beside her, she began again. Finally, she looked up at Seth and told him the whole story.

When she finished, it was obvious that Seth was as shocked as she had been. He had known Ed Royal for years, and he had never seen anything that would have indicated he was a violent man in any way. He was hard in some ways, but Seth had always noticed that he was gentle with the kids, and seemed like a caring man. Although he had never attended church with Grandma, he seemed like a man of faith. It was hard to imagine him murdering his brother or abusing his child. It was just unthinkable. But of course he did not doubt Esther's word.

"I know this is a terrible story to hear," said Seth. "Where do you go from here?"

"I haven't really let the whole story sink in I don't think. Aunt Esther said that from the time that happened, Dad became a different person, that he really lived his life trying to make up for his terrible actions. She said that Grandma never forgave him, though. At least that was the way Esther saw it. She said that Grandma refused to allow him to ever be alone with me, even after I got a little older. Esther said that Grandma seemed to accept his killing Rufus, or at least understand it, but she never understood his beating me. I guess I may have sensed that tension between Grandma and Dad, but I never really remember hearing anything between them. I guess I can be thankful for my grandmother's love and protection. I just feel really sad for all of them, Esther included. I think she has really struggled with whether to tell me the truth. I think she felt that it was the only way I could really heal. But I don't know."

"Do you have an appointment this week with Dr. Adams?" asked Seth.

"No, but I do next week. Should I tell the kids about all this?"

"I don't know. Maybe we should wait until you talk with Dr. Adams. Maybe he can help you decide. On the one hand, it would help them, especially Samuel, to understand why you left, and that might help heal the relationship between you and him. On the other hand, it would be a terrible thing to know about their grandfather."

"Don't you think Samuel is doing much better lately?" asked Katie.

"He is definitely doing better. My concern is that he will continue to question anything you do that he doesn't understand. If he could know the trauma that you went through as a child, it might help to erase his suspicions, knowing that you now understand yourself better."

Seth decided to go to Dr. Adams with Katie for her next visit and listen as she related her whole story to him, and together they would decide how to use the information to help the kids' cope with their mother's actions. In the end it was decided that it would be helpful to give Samuel the whole story, since he was older and was having a much harder time forgiving his mother. And for Abby, they decided to begin by giving her a modified version of events, one that would help her to feel confident that her mother would not leave her again, but would not be too graphic an account of the actual happening. When she was older, they could answer her questions more completely.

After things had been explained to both children, both Katie and Seth saw a big difference in the way Samuel related to his mother. His conversations were much more open and honest, and while he was still sometimes a rebellious middle school boy, it was obvious that he trusted and loved his mother once again. As for Abby, there was not a drastic change, but she continued to grow in her trust and dependence on Katie.

As Katie began to feel safe again, a few long-lost memories began to surface. Most of the time they came as dreams just before she awakened in the mornings, and they were very vivid. In one of her dreams she was sitting inside the barn on some hay, holding a little kitten. She was alone in an empty stall, but she was not afraid because she heard Uncle Rufus and Liz talking at the other end of the barn. Liz had caught the kitten and handed it to her when she saw that Katie was chasing it. Uncle Rufus was fixing something at the other end of the barn and Liz walked on down to where he was as Katie took the kitten into the stall. She was humming a little song she had learned in church to the baby kitten, when she heard her dad come into the barn and yell something. She started to go out to meet him when she realized he was mad so she stayed still. She didn't hear anything for a few minutes and then she heard him start yelling again, this time she could tell he was mad at Uncle Rufus. She slipped up to where the feeding trough was and climbed up on it so that she could see better just as she heard a loud bang, and she saw Liz run out of the barn and back up the road. She saw Rufus fall to the ground at the back end of the barn and saw her dad bend down, and say, "No, no, I didn't mean…" He had blood all over his hands. She ran as fast as she could. Katie awoke in a panic. She remembered the dream vividly, and she realized that what Aunt Esther had said was true. She had been in the barn when her father had shot his brother. Always before, when someone would mention Uncle

Rufus, she had no idea what he looked like except for a few pictures of him as a teenager that Aunt Esther had once shown her. But in her dream, she saw him clearly.

It was several weeks later when she had another very real dream that helped her to understand the washing machine incident. She had done several loads of laundry that day and had fallen asleep on the couch, waiting for Seth to get home. All of a sudden she was a little four-year old girl in a small room looking at a shirt of her dad's. It had blood all over it and there was no one there to wash it. He must hate that Uncle Rufus' blood had spilled on his shirt. The housekeeper had not come today, but Katie had gone to her house for a while. Four-year-old Katie went to the kitchen and lifted the half-full bucket of water off the table and brought it into the little room and poured it into the tub, as she had seen the housekeeper do it. Then she poured some washing powder into the tub and put her dad's shirt into the water, and began rubbing the spots on the washing board as she had seen it done.

"What are you doing, Katie?"

"No! No! Please!" Katie shouted, as she pushed Seth back away from her.

Realizing that she was obviously having a bad dream, Seth backed off, allowing her to get awake and see that it was him.

Looking around with a frightened look on her face, Katie took it all in and then spoke.

"Seth, I just remembered in a dream what I experienced when I was trying to wash my father's shirt. Now it's not just a story that Aunt Esther told me. It's my story."

CHAPTER 23

As Katie approached the now familiar Southeast Medical Center, she said a little prayer that her father would be lucid and willing to talk to her today. She had rehearsed in her head what she had come to say, but her success in communicating with him depended upon his own lucidity.

Betty was seated behind the desk this morning and smiled at her as she approached.

"Katie, it's good to see you. You know, Mr. Royal just asked about you this morning. I think it's the first time he's ever asked about anyone."

"Great. That is exactly what I needed to hear," said Katie, encouraged by the news. She just hoped he still remembered that he had asked.

Betty stepped around the desk. "Could I speak with you a moment before you go back?" she asked.

"Of course." Katie followed her to the far corner of the lobby area, adjusting her purse strap over her shoulder.

"I'm a little concerned about your father. Ever since your last visit, he's been a little edgy and has not been sleeping well. Once he asked me for some pain medicine. When I told him he would have to get that from a doctor, he became very upset and said he had to have something. When I asked him where he hurt, he didn't answer me. Frankly, I'm concerned that he might be suicidal."

"Oh my," said Katie. "What do you think is wrong?"

"That's just it. I don't know. I thought maybe you could provide some insight. Just listen to him today and see if you can help."

"I will." Katie hoped she could help, but her heart raced all the way down the hall and she could hardly hold back her tears.

When Katie pushed open the door to Ed Royal's room, she saw that he was lying on his bed, fully clothed, with his face toward the wall. She entered quietly, closing the door back, and sat down in a chair near the window. He showed no signs of hearing her enter, so she said nothing. Looking out the window, she saw the neatly mowed lawn and the colorful flowers blooming all down the side of the fence that delineated the property of the medical center. The beauty of the world just outside intensified the sadness of the situation for Katie, and tears were streaming down her cheeks before she could stop them. She looked around the room for a tissue, and as she did she saw her father staring at her face.

Suddenly, with no limp or difficulty as he had shown before, Ed Royal arose grabbed a tissue from his bedside table, and was by her side in a second, kneeling down and wiping her face and consoling her. "It's okay, baby," he said. "I won't hurt you again. I love you. I never meant to hurt you."

"Papa!" Katie instinctively wrapped her arms around his neck and continued to sob, and her father began sobbing too. Suddenly she was four years old again and her loving father was consoling her after a fall of some other disappointment. After a long time, Katie pulled away ever so gently and helped him to his feet.

"Let's sit over here, Papa. I have a lot to talk to you about— I sort of wrote out a script. But much of it has already been said now. The main thing I came to tell you is that I love you. I would like to know the whole story from you, but even if I can't hear it from you, I want you to know that I forgive you and that I love you."

Ed Royal's eyes, still wet with tears, stared at his daughter. "But I don't deserve that, Katie. I deserve punishment. I did some terrible things, and the longer I live, the more devastating results will come from my deeds. So maybe when I die, it will stop."

"No, Papa, dying does not stop the consequences; it's forgiveness and reconciliation that can transform people's lives and relieve the pain. When I heard the whole story, I considered all my options, and I came to the conclusion that if I am to be a happy person and a good mother, I had to make peace, not add to the pain."

"So you know what happened to Rufus?"

"Yes."

"And you know what happened to your arm?" he asked, with fear in his eyes.

"Yes, Papa. I know everything."

"And you still love me? I don't understand."

"You made a horrible mistake—two horrible mistakes. But you were also willing to give me up to the care of my grandmother. It was obviously very difficult for you not to be allowed to raise me yourself after having to care for me during the first few years of my life. But you kept your promise and allowed grandmother to make all the decisions for me. So, yes, you made your mistakes, but you are not a totally bad person. I have made some poor choices myself, but I'm trying to make amends too. We can both become better people if we try."

"I'm a lot older than you are, Katie. I just don't see much hope for me."

"Tell me about Liz, Papa. You had a good marriage with her didn't you? Don't you think she'd want you to try to get your life back on track, be a grandfather to Samuel and Abby?"

"Oh, Liz. Poor Liz. How I loved her. She tried to take responsibility for what I did, but of course it wasn't her fault. She was just an innocent girl who got caught up in my obsession and didn't realize she was in a dangerous situation. She was never involved with Rufus in the way I'd imagined. She enjoyed him the same way everyone enjoyed him—he was fun to be around. And I – I was more serious, but Liz knew I loved her and she would never have betrayed me. I guess I knew that in a way, but I was always jealous of Rufus. When she would laugh as this jokes and talk to him, it drove me crazy—literally. I just wish there was some way I could take it all back, but I can't. I hope I can find a way to live with it."

Katie left her father with mixed feelings about him. On the one hand she felt like a load had been lifted from her because she had been able to talk to him and tell him she forgave him. But in another sense, she had a sense of foreboding, a sense that something was not right with him. She kept remembering Betty's mention of his suicidal thoughts, and even his mention to her that he didn't know if he could find a way to live with what he'd done. She couldn't believe that he would take his life though, not after she'd told him she loved him and forgave him. Something was not right though. She realized that she had no idea what his physical condition was. She made a mental note to see if she could get an appointment to talk to the doctor who treated him at the nursing home.

CHAPTER 24

It was spring and Katie loved planting flowers, so she had gone to the seed store and bought several packs of flowers—annuals mostly—to restore her little flower garden which had grown up during her absence the last two years. Saturday morning she put on her gardening clothes—shorts, a tee-shirt, an old pair of gym shoes, a hat, and a pair of work gloves. She couldn't wait to get busy digging in the little garden. It contained good black soil with hardly any rocks. Once she pulled out all the old weeds it was easy digging. As she hummed a familiar song, she saw an unfamiliar blue late model car pull into the driveway. Thinking someone was needing directions, she straightened up, and looked as the tall, neatly dressed woman, looking like she might be in her late fifties, got out of the car and walked up toward the house.

"Are you Katie Royal?" she asked.

"I was Katie Royal, but I'm Katie Johnson now," answered Katie. There was something familiar about the woman, but

Katie couldn't quiet put her finger on it. Was she a relative? Or someone she had known once?

"I'm sorry. That's what I meant," said the woman.

"Who are you? You look sort of familiar. Do I know you?" asked Katie.

"No. Probably not. My name is Ora Mae Fields," she said.

"That's funny. My mother's name was Ora Mae, too, but I never knew her. She left when I was a baby," said Katie.

"I am that same Ora Mae," the woman said, breaking into tears.

"You're...You're my mother?" Katie was overwhelmed. "How did you find me? Where have you been?"

It was several minutes before the woman could compose herself enough to say anything more. Finally, Katie invited her to come up on the porch and sit down. Katie had learned so much about her family the last few months that this seemed to be the final piece to the puzzle of her life. She didn't know what to feel, but she was eager to see what had brought her mother back after all those years.

"Katie dear, I have not come to ask forgiveness for running away, because I know that would be too much. I just wanted to see you, and explain a few things if you are willing to listen. Would you be willing to do that?" Ora Mae asked, looking strikingly like an older version of her daughter, her dark brown hair curling around her face the way Katie's always had.

"I will be glad to listen," said Katie. "I just can't believe you're here. A lot has happened to me in the last few years, and I cannot be the judge of your actions, but I'm willing to listen to your story."

"First of all, I found you because your Aunt Esther found me. She seemed to think you needed to know everything about your past in order to move forward with your own life. Somehow she had a friend to look me up in the Detroit, Michigan, phone book. I'm not sure how it all came about, but she told me a little of what had been going on in your life, and asked if I could come down and visit her so that we could talk about all the events that led up to your leaving home and then returning to your family. I got here yesterday, spent last night with her, and she gave me directions to your house. At first I thought I should call or something, but she just wanted me to come on over. I hope that was okay."

"Aunt Esther knows me well. She knew it would be all right," said Katie. "I can't believe she was able to find you. But she told me that she always liked you, and I suspect that she might have contacted you a long time ago if she had it her way," said Katie.

"Let me give you the short version of my story, and then if you want to know more, I'll give you more. First of all I was very young and somewhat wild when I married Ed. He was a little older and very serious. Before you were born, I had realized that he and I had little in common, and I was like a rebellious teenager wanting to leave home." She stopped for a moment. "I had no idea about what happened between Rufus and Ed. Rufus was always pleasant, and sometimes he was a little flirtatious, but nothing ever happened between us." She sat silently for a few moments, reflecting on the horrible tale Esther had related to her earlier.

"Anyway, I did some very stupid and sometimes dangerous things while you were a baby, the worst of which was to run off with a man who was much worse than Ed ever was. But I was young and I had my pride, so I would have never asked his or his family's help once I left. Initially I went with this man named Jason to Ohio, thinking I would return eventually, but he was so controlling he would not allow it. Eventually I did get away from him. Later I married John and went farther North. John was a kind, protective man. Unfortunately, he seldom had a job and we lived like paupers. Several times we talked about trying to come to get you, but always in the end we knew that you were better off with your dad and Grandma, who always had plenty to eat and a good home. You may wonder why I never contacted you after I left. I tried to contact them twice. The first time I talked to Ed and he told me not to call back. The second time I talked to his mother and she told me the same thing. From what Aunt Esther tells me, I was never mentioned once I left and they did not want her to ask about me."

Ora Mae had a pained expression on her face. "One thing I knew is that you were loved and well-cared for. Ed adored you and so did your grandmother. I remember when I was always leaving the house and coming home late at night or the next morning, he was always so patient with you, and I was often ashamed. I just can't imagine him ever doing anything to hurt you or anyone else." She sighed.

"After I married John, we were never financially able to come back to Kentucky. It was only after he died two years ago that I learned he had a little life insurance policy that he had kept up all those years. It helped me to pay off a few debts, and with my own work keeping books for a small law firm, I'm fairly comfortable now." Ora Mae looked at Katie to see how she was taking all this information. Katie looked at her, not with hatred as Ora Mae probably expected, but kindness and forgiveness.

"Could I call you 'Mother'?" Katie asked. The two women stood and embraced. In her whole life Katie had never called anyone "Mother." Now that her grandmother was gone, she needed a mother. And her mother, never having had any other children, needed a daughter.

"Nothing would please me more," said the older woman.

"I want you to meet Seth and the kids," said Katie. "Could you stay until they get home?"

"I have no other plans," was the response.

After the shock of finding out who was visiting that afternoon, Seth and the kids all seemed to like the idea of having a grandmother in their house. Even Samuel sat down and talked to Ora Mae for a long time, asking her what it was like in Detroit. Before the visit was over, both kids expressed interest in a trip to Michigan next summer.

When Katie left for work Monday morning, she was feeling better about her family situation. She still, however, kept to herself at work and when she went home she did not walk in the neighborhood very often.

She almost had dinner ready that evening when she heard a knock on the door. When she opened the door, there stood Aunt Esther.

"Why, Aunt Esther, how good to see you! You're almost in time for dinner," Katie said. Then she saw the look on the older woman's face and realized something was wrong. "What is it?" she asked.

"Katie, did you go back to see your father since we talked?"

"Why, yes. As a matter of fact, I went—let's see, last Thursday. We had a long talk and I did as you suggested—I told him I forgave him. We had a wonderful visit. But to be honest, I'm a little concerned, and I'm going to see if I can talk to his doctor—"

Katie realized Aunt Esther was trying to interrupt her. "Oh, Katie, your father—he died this morning."

Katie wrapped her arms around Esther and began to cry. "Oh, I just had this feeling—what happened to him?"

"They don't know for sure, but they think he had a massive heart attack," said Esther.

"I think he just couldn't live with what he'd done," said Katie. "When I left him on Thursday, I could tell that he just couldn't forgive himself. I told him I forgave him, and that I loved him. Thank you for encouraging me to do that, Aunt Esther."

"I'm so glad you did, Katie. It will save you and your family. I'm convinced of that."

CHAPTER 25

Within six months after Katie learned of the tragic events of her early childhood, she was beginning to feel that she was really home again with her family. But it was Christmas time the following year when it became true in the school and community.

In early December, Cora Morgan, one of her neighbors, came by one afternoon with a fresh made tin of brownies. "Katie, I wanted to come by and thank you for what you've done for Cole, my grandson, who is in Miss Patton's class. He just loves you and he has gained so much confidence this year. Last year in kindergarten, he was so shy and hated to go to school. Now he can't wait to get to school to see 'Miss Katie.' Thank you!"

"You're welcome. Cole is a wonderful little boy," said Katie.

"Katie, I want to apologize for my part in not making you feel welcomed back," said her neighbor. "Brenda told me that there were some things in your past that you were not aware of at the time. She didn't go into what they were, but most of us

223

have some unresolved 'skeletons' in our closets, and sometimes we forget that those things can cause actions we don't understand. I know it's been hard work for you to try to uncover some of those things and I wish I had been more supportive."

"I understand. When I returned here, I mostly felt that I deserved whatever happened to me anyway, so I accepted it as my just punishment I guess."

"We're having a little Christmas party at our house next Saturday evening for the people in the neighborhood, and we'd love to have your family there," she said.

"I'll have to check with Seth, but I think we can come," Katie said. At that moment she felt like she had come full circle and was home again. If she could ever get a teaching job back, she would really be back home in her profession as well. But that would take time.

The night of the party, excitement was in the air. It was a family party, and the kids were all out playing in the two inches of snow which had already fallen. They were predicting another two inches before morning. It was a good night to be doing something on the street, where no one had to drive. Seth and Katie had promised to bring some brownies and a pecan pie. Katie liked the brownies to be warm, so she had taken them out of the oven only thirty minutes before they were to go to the party. As they left the house, the snow was falling and the street looked like pictures Katie had seen on Christmas cards. Houses were aglow with strings of colored lights, and decorated trees were visible through windows or doors of most of the houses. Children were skating, sledding or throwing snowballs on several snow-covered lawns. The beauty of the scene around her gave Katie a good feeling.

Despite the pleasant surrounding beauty, however, Katie admitted to Seth that she felt a little anxious, since this was really the first time she had been involved in a community gathering since her return. Both Cora, who was having the party, and her friend Brenda Jackson assured her that she was welcome, she could not help but feel a little nervous. Seth put his free arm around her shoulders, shifting the pecan pie to his other hand. "It's going to be fine," he assured her. Bolstered by his support, she stepped more confidently as they walked up the driveway to the Morgan's front door.

Cora opened the door just as they were about to ring the doorbell. "Come in, come in," she invited them. "Let me take your coats. I think your kids are already in our back yard constructing a snow man under the lights out there."

After introducing them to a couple of new neighbors, Cora was leading them to the tables laden with food when a familiar voice spoke Katie's name. Brenda Jackson appeared from behind her followed by Katie's one-time co-worker Julie McFadden. They both greeted Katie and Seth warmly, and Seth took the brownies from Katie and placed them on the table at the other end of the dining room. Katie looked around at Cora's beautifully decorated home. Christmas music drifted from the living room as guests talked and moved from one room to another. She began to relax as she accepted some hot cider from Cora and picked up a cookie from one of the plates. She and Seth visited with some of the neighbors and she met another new couple from the next street over.

Jeannie, one of her neighbors whose son was Samuel's age appeared from the next room and gave her a hug. "Katie, I'm so glad to see you again! You look great."

"Thanks, I feel great, too," said Katie truthfully.

"Listen, I wanted to ask you something. A few of us were thinking about starting a little book group of people close by. Julie suggested that maybe we might get you to sort of lead it since you are an English teacher, and have probably read a lot more than most of us have. Would you consider it?" she asked.

"When were you planning to meet?" asked Katie.

"Well, we were thinking either one evening, or maybe even on a weekend. We really hadn't set a time, but we're flexible." Jeannie said, looking toward the living room door as Julie entered. "Julie, I was asking Katie about the book club idea. Were you thinking a weekday evening, or the weekend."

"Either one would be fine with me," Julie said. "What about you, Katie?"

"Well, I could probably do either one, but of the weekdays, Thursdays are usually better for me," said Katie. "Most of the time the kids don't have much homework on Thursday nights, so things are a little easier."

"When do we want to meet and get a plan?" asked Julie, looking at the other two.

Brenda walked up about that time, "Get a plan for what?"

"A book club. Want to join?" asked Jeannie. "Katie has agreed to lead it—I think—haven't you?" She looked at Katie.

"I'll give it a try, but since you've already discussed it, you'll need to tell me at the planning meeting what you want me to do," said Katie.

"Why don't we meet the first Thursday in January, which will be the 5th, I believe? Is that okay with all of you?" asked Jeannie.

"Sounds good to me," said all the girls at the same time.

As Jeannie and Brenda turned and began to talk to others, Julie stayed and talked to Katie, telling her a little about what was going on with the other teachers.

"Katie, I haven't seen much of you since you've been working with Miss Patton this year, but I wish you'd come up to our end of the hall and get to know some of the new teachers. I know it's a little awkward for you, but I think you'd be surprised at how you'll be received. Anyway, I'm not really supposed to say anything, but I think it's possible you might get a teaching job again next fall. Don't tell anyone that I mentioned it though," Julie finished.

"What makes you think that?" asked Katie.

"Well, nothing specific, but I know there'll be an opening," said Julie. "And I heard Carl make a comment to the assistant principal which I was not supposed to hear. He didn't call your name, but I know he was meaning you. He just said 'Now that we know the truth about her, I think she deserves another chance,' or something like that. I just acted as if I didn't hear him. Anyway, I would just like for you to get to know everyone this spring whether you get the job or not."

By the end of the party Katie was exhausted, but happy. After saying goodnight to their host and hostess, she and Seth got their dishes and headed back up the street behind the kids. Now the street was quieter but still beautiful, and the snow was still falling. Holding onto Seth's arm with her free hand, Katie looked up into the falling snow and said, "I am reminded of a sentence I read by Hal Borland the other day. It said, 'To know after absence the familiar street and road and village and house is—' "

" 'to know again the satisfaction of home.'" Seth finished the sentence for her.

She smiled at his familiarity with the quote. "I was thinking that there's a lot more involved in feeling at home than just being in familiar territory though. You know, I've been back for several months now, but I think this is the first time I've really felt at home."

ABOUT THE AUTHOR

Merrill Johnson Davies has been writing and publishing most of her life. Beginning in high school in Southeastern Kentucky as feature editor of *The Hazel Nut*, and continuing throughout her thirty-one years of teaching high school English, she has always enjoyed writing and teaching writing. When she retired from teaching in 2003, she began to focus more on her efforts to write fiction. *The Welsh Harp*, her first novel, was published in 2012. *The Truth About Katie* is her second novel.

In addition to writing, Merrill is active in Toastmasters, The Georgia Council of Teachers of English, the National Council of Teachers of English, and her church. She also enjoys spending time with her husband and two daughters and their families, including six grandchildren. Merrill and her husband Bill live in Rome, Georgia.